STORIES TO HIDE FROM YOUR MOTHER

STORIES TO HIDE
FROM YOUR MOTHER

TESS FRAGOULIS

ARSENAL PULP PRESS
Vancouver

ARSENAL PULP PRESS
103-1014 Homer Street
Vancouver, B.C.
Canada V6B 2W9

The publisher gratefully acknowledges the support of the Canada
Council for the Arts for its publishing program, and the support
of the Book Publishing Industry Development Program, and the
B.C. Arts Council.

The following stories were previously published: "Tatterdemalion
Bride" (*Blood and Aphorisms* and *Stories from Blood and Aphorisms,* Gutter Press); "How to Pick Up Women" (*McGill Street
Magazine* and *Matrix*); "Hair in the Mousetrap" (*Canadian Fiction Magazine*); "Exhortations" (*McGill Street Magazine*).

Typeset by the Vancouver Desktop Publishing Centre
Printed and bound in Canada

CANADIAN CATALOGUING IN PUBLICATION DATA:
Fragoulis, Tess.
  Stories to hide from your mother

  ISBN 1-55152-045-1

  I. Title.
PS8561.R238S76 1997   C813'.54   C97-910923-X
PR9199.3.F66S7 1997

CONTENTS

EXHORTATIONS

"... if a certain individual is a painter, you think he is a very original artist, but let that man be the cashier of a big bank and the bank will experience something. They will say that fellow is surely crazy."

—C.G. JUNG

GENTLE BUREAUCRATS:
    I would like to receive your grant to complete a collection of short stories entitled *Stories To Hide From Your Mother*, of which I have enclosed four. The stories are a series of random outpourings that nobody's mother should read, let alone mine. "Your parents don't belong in your bedroom," my therapist says, and I'm relieved. I have no problem, however, letting other people read about my secret perversions and peccadilloes, people who don't know me and were not in my gym class when I was twelve, on the day the cool girls caught me with tissues stuffed down my shirt.

Breastless girls got no respect in high school—not from the boys, not from the other girls whose glands kick-started early. Why I imagined I could just wad up tissues and stuff them down my pukey yellow gym shirt without the help of even a training bra, I don't know. I refuse to make any excuses for the follies and misjudgments of youth. Of course, the breasted girls (how I hated them) nailed me immediately. "She stuffs," the leader of the endowed confirmed with an assured nod. The incriminating whisper travelled around the room like the lit fuse on a cartoon stick of dynamite. It negotiated the periphery of the semi-circle in which we sat to listen to the gym teacher's confused ramblings about menstruation, pregnancy, and personal hygiene until the accusation reached me. Everyone was staring at my chest, and the girl next to me extended a finger, poked my right falsie, and laughed. Everyone else started laughing in that expressionistic, horrifying manner, where all the ridiculed person sees is crooked, open mouths, pointing fingers, and funhouse-mirror faces. Red-faced, but still feigning ignorance, I looked down at my chest and noticed that my left wad of tissue had shimmied down to my belly button. With all the dignity I could muster, I excused myself from the class without any attempt to move the wad back into its place. I don't know what was said after I exited, or I've conveniently blocked out the rumours that circulated for the rest of the year. I never went back to that gym class, lying to the school nurse instead, telling her that I had asthma while I wheezed and banged on my flat chest with my fist.

Probably none of those girls remember that incident today, whereas I wish them all ill health, saggy breasts, bad jobs, delinquent children, and abusive husbands. Beyond the ample bosom I have since developed without the help of surgical procedures, I obviously still have something of my self-worth to recover. The grant would be a good start.

How I will keep these stories from my mother once the collection is published is another matter entirely, one that keeps me up at night, interferes with my breathing, and sometimes cramps up my writing hand. My therapist says I should just confront Mother about punishing me for playing kissing games in the alleyway when I was thirteen, and this whole need to hide would disappear. But I'm not ready yet. I've decided not to think about it for the time being, and my life would be perfect if only the damn nightmares would go away.

The other night, for instance, I dreamt I was naked and having sex with a famous film director (who shall remain nameless, and should not be confused with the person who wrote my letter of recommendation) on my mother's black-and-green-striped couch. The TV was tuned into some shopping channel that was selling off an overstock of tri-coloured dildos, which looked like those red, white, and blue rocket popsicles. They were also pushing a brand of erotic massage oil that made your skin burst into flames from the friction. "Exactly what I want to feel like," I told the director, "a full body yeast infection." He reprimanded me for always talking dirty during the act, but not in the right way; he said it was distracting. I told him it didn't distract me at all and, in fact, kept my mind off of whether I was going to have an orgasm or not because when I think about it too seriously I get sidetracked by my own thoughts and desires, then I get too anxious and I don't have one. By this point he was moaning and groaning, since I'd managed to keep the rhythmic thrust of my pelvis going to the beat of my words, which in the dream came out as a sonnet. He was kneading my breasts like wet clay, licking my face like a rocket popsicle and, suddenly, I felt it, too: the contraction and the swelling, the tickle that grows exponentially until it consumes my whole body and makes me twist, grind, and contort slavishly in service to its panic. I was about to reach climax when the door swung open and my mother walked in holding a naked rag doll out towards me, its painted-on heart shining and throbbing like that of a holographic Jesus. I woke up with a jolt, my hand buried in my underwear, my breathing strained, my whole body shaking, and the moment lost. I felt frustrated, unable to write for the rest of the day, though I did manage to record the dream for the purposes of this proposal.

I realize that it is a little premature to be worrying about that day when Mother sees a dozen copies of the book in a shop window, stacked in a neat pyramid, my face smiling intelligently in black-and-white from the back cover. Or that awful moment when she picks up the nearest telephone, jabs indignantly at the push buttons with a fingernail painted Fuschia Punch, and says nothing when I answer, but breathes harshly and expects me to start spewing excuses/apologies/explanations. Which I will. I do not yet have publishers tripping over themselves to purchase the collection. Nor are any high-powered agents buying me expensive lunches in quaint but impressive bistros, where all the fantastically-attired patrons speak in hushed tones and look around to see who's watching them.

The stories have not been sent around yet because I live in isolation. Not in the sense of someone who is in prison and could never hope for a government grant. (Though an actual inmate would probably be in a better position to pay for the postage required to send her scribblings on the many excursions necessary to seduce a publisher, considering her lack of everyday expenses and the salary collected from banging out license plates. Not to mention the spare time—glorious time.) I am imprisoned by newness. I am trapped in the unknown.

I know you'll say that every famous writer started there, and that, somehow, if I persist, if I give up evenings at the opera, transcontinental love affairs, the peace of mind of a regular paycheque, and any hope of evading the delirium that sets in after spending too much time wading knee-deep in the bilge of my own brain, I will one day be allowed to leave that dark place—that savage land stalked by bosses in bad suits who obsess over stapling procedure (horizontal, not diagonal), and fire you for doing personal work on their computer. For the record, it wasn't my fault that the minister said the word "pubic" instead of "public" in his speech to the nation. There was a lot of flak and talk of conspiracy and wrong-doing, but really it was just an oversight, and quite absurd and even funny if you take a minute to think about it. It had absolutely nothing to do with my personal work or my proclivities, as was insinuated in the internal memo. I was pressed for time, and I'm no typist of any merit, so I was running my fingers over the keyboard as fast as they would go and somehow I missed the *l*. So sue me. One measly letter. Even the spell-check missed it, and in my humble opinion there is nothing whatsoever wrong with our government coming up with a policy on "Pubic Health."

At the hearing there were all sorts of allegations about my spending suspicious amounts of time in washrooms on other floors, and about my crossing my legs too tightly at my desk. The office manager had broken into my computer and retrieved two of my stories that have detailed descriptions of "genitalia and the uses thereof," as it was put in the official transcripts. A paranoid supervisor from another department, a tall/skinny/ugly/man who didn't like women, even suggested that I might be a spy, an infiltrator from the opposition sent in to make the minister look ridiculous. "Well, you don't need me for that," I blurted out, unable to contain myself under the strain. This sealed my fate—insubordination—and, except for the severe reduction in funds and the now constant presence of canned herring in my diet, I am as happy to be rid of them as they are of me. I hope that this little incident doesn't affect my application. I thought I would mention it of my own accord, explain my side of the story so the jury won't have to contend with some bastardized version scrawled on the walls of government washrooms. I'd like to get in there some day with a thick red marker and set things straight.

But until I have found my own key to the literary executive washroom, you'll say, I cannot expect a government agency to legitimize my existence. That's not what government agencies are for. They are there to confirm legitimacy where it already exists. This might explain the national deficit: work done in duplicate, paper clips stolen by employees.

I don't feel that giving me the grant, instead of my doddering old professor—who put in a topiary garden at his country house with his last one—would legitimize me. It would just give me the opportunity to do the work necessary towards acquiring that key. You see, I was too young to say anything meaningful or original in university, that socially sanctioned time to be self-indulgent and to find my voice. It just didn't happen, though the student loan still haunts me.

There were too many life things to explore, too many bedraggled professors looking down my shirt and inviting me out for late night drinks in smoky cafés, reciting poems they said I inspired. The words *nymph, sylph,* and *fay* recurred in their verses as if the men had huddled gnomishly in a dusty corner of the faculty lounge to come up with a strategy that would drug me like fairy dust. What they were not aware of as they plotted was my propensity as a child to squish lightning bugs between my palms when I clapped to revive Tinkerbell. Unfortunately, this type of irony was beyond my grasp at twenty-one, so I spent my days writing autobiographical sketches with loosely disguised characters, ultimately revealing the ordinariness of my life to the world. The professors, their egos stroked by my attention to their prowess, encouraged me to keep writing in the same vein, while patting my knee under the desk. There were no prizes in the classroom for slicing open a blood vessel and bleeding all over your paper, for revealing any personal truth or style, so I didn't. Who can be a Dostoevsky, a Barthelme, a Beckett at twenty-one, anyway?

Everyone knows that a writer doesn't come into her own until middle age, but you don't just start then. You've got to indulge fastidiously to get there. You've got to lie in bed staring at the spider webs on the ceiling until noon and questioning the meaning of life and your place in the grand scheme of things—daily. Stay up until three a.m. drinking cheap rum, straight up, and making raspy, long-distance phone calls to men who no longer love you because you're too absorbed in the writing you're going to do—someday. Wait impatiently for the time to pass, watching sitcoms and eating chocolate bars for comfort, until you turn forty and people begin to take you seriously—you hope. These things take time. And money.

I've tried working full-time and writing on the side, but I don't know how anyone can produce anything under such oppressive conditions. First, to stay close to my trade, I worked for a publishing company where I was severely underpaid and not up for promotion. To add insult to injury, I had to travel two hours a day on public transit to get there and to engage in shoving matches for seats with pubescent girls with acne, attitude, and no sense of proportion, let alone humour.

I then got a contract with the aforementioned government department, where I was forced to feed reams of dead wood through the fax machine. The messages I sent were mostly meaningless, such as, "The announcement that we were expecting to announce this morning will not be announced until this afternoon." I'd sit there for hours on end—the office delinquent banished to the corner—staring at the machine sucking in and spitting out wasted paper until my eyes and brain bugged out. At both jobs I was tortured by rotund office women who yammered to me about their weight problems all day long, though none were prepared to become starving artists or to offer me their second cranberry muffin. Not surprisingly, during these two periods, my ability to write disappeared.

These were the dark days of illicit drugs and love. Of self-loathing and despair. Of Nietzsche and Sylvia Plath—a combination as lethal as downers and razor blades. I don't know what kept me alive except for the dream that perhaps someday I would receive a government grant, and my life would become a surreal circus with shooting stars and fireworks; with three-headed lions purring and rubbing their wet noses against my calf; and with stilt men showering me with sparkles and gumdrops as I walked the tightrope in a form-fitting, sequined garment to my magic computer, which had the power to transform my every thought and whim into beauteous and meaningful prose, the likes of which had never been meant before.

But I am ready now. Renewed, rarin' to go. I have been unemployed for six glorious months and working on my collection as often as I have had the psychological energy and the nerve. I have turned out the first four stories and believe that even though in ten years time I may not want to acknowledge their existence, I am entering my phase of Important Work. Important to me, anyway. And the comments, so far, have been favourable from those willing to take the ride.

Did I mention that I've had to start two separate businesses to support my habit? One is an editorial service for illiterate students where I whip hopeless term papers into shape, and then shake my head in dismay as I overcharge for the overhaul. The second is a historical singing telegram service where I compose bawdy verses then deliver them clad in a medieval maiden's outfit, my ample bosom pushed up to my chin with wire, string, and tape. I bounce around happily when I sing to distract the recipient from my inability to carry a tune. The second one, at least, gets me out of the house, and has even landed me a few dates. I worry, however, that these sidelines will take me away from my Important Work.

I don't know why, on the pay equity scale, this collection weighs in as more valuable than my other endeavours, worthy enough to risk incurring the wrath of my mother, which should not be underestimated. According to my therapist, I have some sort of neurotic, wish-fulfillment, self-esteem motif circling the periphery of my writing, which may very well go back to the bra-stuffing incident. And that need for redemption in itself—unfulfilled, unsatis-fied—would be enough to drive anyone crazy, whatever her fetish might be. (I wonder if aspiring plumbers feel this way?)

If you are going to save one person from derangement, despair, and psychotic episodes—which should be the goal of every government agency—why not save me? I'm a good sort. I give quarters to bums on street corners when it's too cold to be questioning whether they'll use them for food or booze, I help old ladies carry their grocery bags home, and I always vote.

I challenge you to read my stories with open mind and free spirit. Let whatever touches you touch you, laugh out loud if you feel like it, and try to resist the urge to immediately compare my manuscript to the millions of books that have been written throughout history, or even to the last hundred things you've read today. Let the newness sink in, and then make your decision. Newness and risk are good for the soul, for the collective unconscious of a culture. That's what my therapist says, and she charges $100 an hour, so she should know.

You may very well be handing out grants for this type of project, left and right, three years down the line—sort of like sending food to starving desert nations after they're already vulture·bait. But imagine how revolutionary it would be to give me the grant now, when no one else has thought of it. Before I'm famous or dead or lauded by the Americans. Before the cheap paperbacks embossed with tawdry, red-clad bimbos on silver backing are available at major airports and bus stations. And you, whichever one of you argues on my behalf, hangs the jury, pressurizes the most adamant fence-sitter into voting on my behalf—for innocence, for acquittal, for the key—could even get the credit for the keen-eyed discovery. If you act now, that is.

Simply, if you give me the grant, you will help me live my life doing what it is I believe I am here to do. If you cannot find it in your hearts and minds to read this happily, without bias to my predicament in the land of the unknown, without staring impolitely at the barbed-wire scratches all over my face and legs from my many attempts to scale the massive wall of indifference, or at the gunshot wounds through my hands and feet from the moments where I almost made it, then dignity would force me to withdraw my request quietly. Or if I am too late for retreat, to insulate myself against possible rejection by telling everyone I know that I don't believe in the system and that being accepted would mean that I sold my soul to some demon. What does a government agency know about "real" art, anyway? I have heard others use this argument successfully. In the meantime, I will continue to work on my collection in fits and spurts, between my two businesses, my flamenco lessons, and my periods of serious self-doubt.

Incidentally, I've started combining the snake-like hand movements with the continuous foot stamping, but my technique still needs work and I've got the longest arms in the entire class, which makes me self-conscious, though my instructor assures me it's an advantage—like having a bigger gun. I don't like it when my classmates watch me stumble, but some day I hope to be able to stamp my way over to a handsome señor's table, clap my hands determinedly, passionately, coil my snake-like arms around his neck, and hang on until he is out of breath. At least one of my characters may be able to do it. As it turns out, that's what everything is for me—rehearsal for my characters, fodder for a thousand lives.

My story, the only one I really live, is the one in which I write. The character who is I sits at her desk until her butt is sore. She turns off the phone, bolts the door shut, and banishes the lovers and friends who siphon her energy like greedy bats. While the rest of the world is out dancing in the streets, revelling in the moment, in being alive, she is alone at home, digging, recording, rewriting, and cursing her fate. But every once in a while something miraculous happens, and she is momentarily freed of her insecurity and resentment. She quickly gathers her guts and wits in a silk pouch, hangs it around her neck by a golden rope, and writes unfettered until all her words find a beautiful place to live. All she really needs is for someone to notice, to tell her it's okay to go on, or to confirm that she's on the right track. Is that asking too much?

Regardless of how this turns out, rest assured that I will keep writing; I have no choice in the matter. Though I may occasionally feel a little bitterness when other citizens, more readily understandable and socially-connected than I, wave their government cheques at me like red capes at a bullfight. Forgive me if I gore one or two of them with my horns. I'm working on expressing my rage.

In closing, I thank you for taking the time to read my stories and to consider me for these most valued prizes—time and space. I sincerely hope you enjoy the fruits of my insanity, and I look forward to your reply.

And one last request. Please don't tell my mother.

Hair in the Mousetrap

I HAD HAIR THAT YOU COULD tear off in clumps when I was a little girl. Long, tangled webs which other children yanked at on the school bus home. My mother did her best to tame the mess, but when she pulled the comb through it, I always cried.

Once, in a sandbox by a hill where a train went by, a little boy I was playing with threw handfuls of wet sand at me. Misplaced affection. I blamed the lice I got on the sand and not on him. My mother knew better. She bought this delousing shampoo that smelled like varsol and stung like soap in your eyes. Every night for the next two weeks, we played out a ritual where repentance was wreaked on my flesh.

She would drag me, kicking and screaming, to the bathtub. She then trapped me in mother stocks: one large hand grasping both my wrists behind my back, while the other hand poured the bug-killing juice all over my cringing scalp. I begged and begged for forgiveness, for mercy, but the expurgation continued until I was pure again, and contrite.

I never went back to that sandbox, and I never played with that little boy again. I wasn't allowed. I never even told her he'd kissed me.

There were always children I wasn't allowed to play with.

My mother considered their parents riff-raff, or she had heard them using bad grammar—things she thought I'd catch. The day I cracked my skull open on monkey bars that belonged to a boy I wasn't supposed to be playing with started a lie that lasted twenty-five years.

Hole in my head, blood matting my hair, unable to reach the doorbell to my grandmother's apartment, I nevertheless had time to make up a lie. I didn't think a cracked skull would grant me immunity for being in the wrong place at the wrong time, so I told my grandmother that I had run, head first, into the metal fence in the alleyway. Better to seem stupid.

My grandmother calmly set a paper towel on my head like a doily on a coffee table, and told me to hold it in place with my hand to blot the blood. She then led me to the fence, roll of paper towels in hand, and had me run through an enactment of the accident before she would take me to the hospital. I quickly added a game of British Bulldog to my story, explaining the procedure of running like a mad person towards a crouching "it," and then heaping yourself on a pile of bodies until the "it" collapsed, suffocated, and died. My Olympian leap overshot the mountain of bodies, I continued, waving my one free hand dramatically, "and that's how I crashed, head first, Grandma, into the fence." She looked at the fence and then at the whites of my eyes, screwed up her mouth in half-belief, laid another paper towel on my head, and hailed a cab.

They were a tough lot, my family. Grandma once told me that if I swallowed hair, a spider would form in my stomach. This horrified me, itinerant strands constantly blowing into my mouth. With the length of my hair, I was sure to produce one of those evil daddy long-legs, dust with pincer limbs, as delicate and frail as hair that breaks off in clumps.

I imagined spiders crawling up my insides whenever I had

an itch. I would pinch myself and slap my skin because I was afraid they'd lay eggs in me and that their offspring would stream out of my ears if someone kissed me. My grandmother didn't tell me that last part; it was what I had learned from experience.

A daddy long-legs made its way up my bedroom wall one afternoon. No one else was at home, and I was afraid I'd released it in my sleep in a teenaged dream I could not remember, but which had left me tense and tender. I dragged the vacuum cleaner down the hall to my room and aimed the tube at the spider, sucking it into oblivion. A fine solution, I thought, until I calculated: one live spider added to a dustbag full of stray hairs (my mother and I both had the same garden-variety, long, stringy locks), equalled the perfect breeding-ground for an army of spiders that would multiply, divide into groups, and conquer the household. Perhaps it was because the daddy long-legs was the only man in the family that I knew we were surely in trouble now. I dropped the dustbag into the building's incinerator without guilt. Patricide. I would accept the punishment.

But punishment in our house was perpetual guilt that swung back and forth like metal balls on thread, increasing in intensity with each collision. Mother could look at me in a way that induced confession, no matter how well-rehearsed my alibi—an oblong stare, a slow, disappointed shake of the head. A daughter will, nevertheless, do what she must do to grow and deal with the consequences later.

I hid a brass stool, a flashlight, and a notepad in the back of my closet. This was my safehouse where I could go to live out my guilt, formulate my excuses and the tone of my confessions. In the darkness, amidst the skirt hems and hanging arms and legs of my wardrobe, I felt safe, sinless, free to touch myself in those forbidden places where hands were slapped away by grandmothers and mothers who threatened their children with blindness, insanity, and hellfire.

I came home from school one day and found my closet door open and my clothes piled upon my bed like the lifeless bodies of fire victims. The bottom of my closet was empty as if scourged by flame, and there were thick arches of plaster smeared onto the walls. My brass stool, flashlight, and notebook were nowhere to be seen, and a lingering cloud of chemicals burned my eyes, sending me running out of the room for air. An exterminator had been in my most private of places, his plaster-dust footprints leading out of my closet to the front door. My mother said she'd discovered mice living among us, diseased vermin that got in through my closet. They had to be eliminated. She never said a word about the notebook, but she continued to stare like a predator, waiting to catch me off guard.

I never saw a mouse either dead nor alive in that room, though I shook my boots out daily before putting them on, and I listened at the walls for them, tapping a rhythm in warning, hoping they'd escape my fate. It was only recently, in my new apartment, that I experienced the violence of suppression firsthand: assorted mouse innards spilling out of an overturned trap baited with bacon. This took place in my bedroom.

I wanted to buy the friendly, environmentally-sound, we're-all-creatures-of-the-earth trap, which catches the mouse live in a metal box with a trap door. I pictured myself letting the mouse out in an open field to run free with its liberated mouse mates, but the box was too expensive, and I live downtown, so the mouse would deteriorate slowly, its spirit broken, its will to live crippled. It would refuse the scraps of food offered through the tiny air holes, waiting in agitation for the guillotine to slice through the air, not believing there was a way out of the darkness. It would probably take its own life by the time I saw the light of a country day. And I couldn't live with it; its presence made me feel dirty, worse than the spiders, as if its warm-blooded body was bloated with my worst secrets. It knew too much.

So I just took a contract out on it: $1.29 and a piece of rotten bacon. Smack and it's over. I even had the body removed by three men I'd picked up on the city streets. I feared the decapitated rodent more than I feared the hairy-chested, cleft-chinned strangers in the bedroom of my over-priced mousebox of an apartment. It was like watching my own death in a dream. One of the strangers refused to leave.

The walls of my box are the blue of a midnight sky. This was my only contribution; everything else has been provided, imposed. Heirlooms, inherited from my grandmother, cover all surfaces: precise needlepoint landscapes and yellowing photographs of sober-faced women in ancient dress, their hair held back tightly in buns. A fly is trapped between the glass and the face of one of the women, its crushed body imitating the dark mole that identifies our line.

The oriental rug on the floor is from my mother's dowry, bought by her grandmother. Its intricate designs describe myths and tragedies in hieroglyphic patterns: Arachne, Clytemnestra, Kore. The dirt ground into its pile is evidence of the lives lived before I was born, the histories that my mother and grandmother conceal—their relations with men. I trample the rug with muddy boots and fingerpaint new dirt into its tableau, to leave my mark, to raise the dead and chase them out of my space. But there's nowhere for them to go, except to slither into the cracks between the walls and floor, like roaches and mice fleeing the light.

Incense and candles burn eternally, filling the room with the thick silence of a temple; inviting, comforting, womblike. There is a door to come in but no way out. That's the trick. That is how I got trapped. That is how I trap. It has been proven in laboratory tests that mice kept in close quarters will fornicate ceaselessly until they die. I have stared at the ceiling of my box, wishing I were dead, while another captive fell into the mania of keeping and feeling alive—photographs of my mother and grandmother watching me with disdain from the mantelpiece.

I have attached extra locks to my door against further intrusion, but sometimes, unconsciously, I unlock them at night. I've laced the corners with poisoned bait, and rigged booby traps at all entry points, loaded with cheese morsels, perfume, and knives. There are condoms by my bedside to protect me from pestilence. These are unnecessary measures. No one has tried to get in for the longest time. I just wait. For the infestation, for the plague, for the trap to come crashing down on my head. This waiting is even more unnerving.

Every once in a while, a mouth presses up against my bedroom window and whispers sweet nothings into my ears, which are pointed towards all sound. I listen for clues, trying to read through to the real meaning behind the words, promising and poisonous at the same time. Slow, tasty lies that momentarily fill me with languor, that make my lips twitch, my stomach rumble.

But I'm not dead yet. I have resisted the temptation to devour what has been offered, to be devoured. I learned early on how to keep away crabs and lice with pure white vinegar, how to shave myself down and dowse the itch. Slash and burn.

Wisdom passed down from mother to daughter. I admire my own ability to abstain.

When I close my eyes I dream of that bumpy ride in the back seat of a car. Of that first ray of sunlight that will blind me for an instant when the trap door is opened, the waft of wild flowers and the taste of fresh air that's just air, which I gulp down hungrily. I can feel the tall grass pressed under my bare feet as I skip through the field looking for others like me to compare passage. I imagine that first sight through squinted eyes of open, endless space. Nothing to wash or comb or vacuum. No one to answer to but mother nature. And I am clean-shaven, hairless, and naked as a pink baby mouse. Happy.

A hand strokes my head and I bolt upright in my bed, panting for air, desperately pushing the hair out of my eyes, scraping it off my tongue with my fingernails. My arms flail in all directions, slapping at my skin to keep the spiders in check. I hear sizzling and metal utensils clanging on pots in the next room. The aroma of bacon frying snakes its way into my bedroom, into my nostrils, and I cower behind my dresser, my head buried in my lap, my breasts pressed into my thighs, sticky with residue, like flypaper. I try to remember when he entered and how, but my brain won't yield the information. My booby traps are tossed indignantly into a corner, their bait crushed underfoot into the oriental rug.

I make a run for the door, but it won't open. I knew that. I've tried before, but I've never been so close, so weakened by hunger. He comes back into the room, tray in hand. I am cornered and foaming at the mouth. I wipe the spittle on the hair of my arm. There's no escape now. I have no other choice. I lunge, attack, shriek like a banshee, hoping to make him run for his life. The words burst out of my mouth like a thousand spiders:

"If you think a measly piece of bacon is going to be enough to entice me you're wrong bucko so you stayed for breakfast big deal you're not the first you think that means you can just move right in and start killing my mice and spiders and bringing me flowers and then when you're tired of me or feeling trapped or unsure of your intentions your sexuality our corresponding biorhythms you can just leave and then I'll have to adjust to all that death and darkness all over again by myself?

"I wouldn't know what to do with you there are no men in my lineage except for the daddy long-legs and I sucked him up my cunt where he multiplies when I sleep and if you go ahead and kiss me because I'm sexy when I'm raving all the spiders I've been harbouring will pour out of my ears like moonrock lava and we'll both be eaten alive by an itch that will never subside."

The very sight of him makes my skin crawl. I stop myself from scratching, not wanting to touch off an eruption. He doesn't even flinch. He smiles as he slowly pushes the tray across the floor towards me. I fold myself in half and escape through a crack in the wall. When I re-emerge, he has gone.

When I turned sixteen, I took myself to a salon and got my hair chopped off, with no one's permission. I clamped my lips shut through the whole operation and then ran to the salon washroom to rinse my mouth out with soap. But I still woke up in the middle of the night, scratching that soft, hairless area of my inner thighs. When my ears buzzed, I imagined it was a spider ringing the doorbell to get out, reminding me that I hadn't let anyone kiss me in a while and the troops were getting restless.

Eat or be eaten. He comes back with an armload of lice traps, spider traps, mouse traps, roach traps, ant traps, earwig traps, silverfish traps, termite traps, beetle traps, bug spray, poison pellets, bottles of vinegar, and a straight razor, and dumps them at my feet. He drags me into the bathroom by my tail, and I nip at his ankles while alternately cursing him and pleading for mercy. He pushes me into the tub and firmly locks my wrists behind my back with his hand. A blow to the back of my knees unhinges them and I kneel on the cold enamel of the tub, my head bowed in prayer, in penance. Warm water rushes over my body and my hairs stand on end. I count the droplets dripping off my nose like rosary beads. With even, sweeping strokes, he glides the razor over my arms, back, neck, breasts, conducting the blade over my body like a cold metal symphony, removing even the invisible hairs around my nipples, the down in the whitest small of my back. He is gentlest when he shaves between my legs, pulling the skin up towards my belly, parting me in half and carefully removing one hair at a time without the slightest scratch. He runs his tongue over my new smoothness and his saliva stings my raw flesh. He let go of my wrists long ago, but I do not stand or try to escape, instead I prostrate myself on the cold enamel, feeling the chill of his breath on my wetness.

He carries me out to the kitchen, spreads me onto the table like a cloth, sprinkles me with salt, and starts to eat. My open pores wince. I make one more feeble attempt to attack, propping myself up on my elbows, but I'm tired and dizzy, and the saliva flowing freely from my mouth slows down my words, makes them go around in circles:

"The bacon smells real good, sitting there on the edge of

your plate, but I nearly didn't make it through the last breakfast, and even though it's been a bumpy ride between you and
me, I don't know that I really believe that the trap door to
this contraption will ever open, but I do believe in spiders and
have learned to live with them in complicity, so stop waving
that bacon in my face, I really don't want any, you see my
mother told me that I shouldn't play with you, and my
grandmother will want to know where I've been if I come
home bleeding, and even though I can now reach her doorbell,
the humiliation will be the same, and that bacon smells real
good sitting there on the edge of your plate."

Maybe a little bite off the side won't hurt, a nibble really,
or maybe just a lick. I'm starting to see him through webs. I
don't know why I'm crying; it must be the spiders scratching
the backs of my eyes. They want to come out. I want to come
out. He says he wants to live here. With me and my vermin.
My father didn't even live with me, and my mothers would
have to approve, and they never do. My ears are ringing like
church bells at midday. He offers a bite. First a kiss, I say, the
bite is inevitable.

He grabs me by my nape and pulls me towards him. Our
lips touch and he passes me the bacon with his teeth. The
spiders cascade over us and we disappear under a blanket of
black snow. A train blows its horn in the distance. I take the
bacon between my teeth and pull. Smack, and it's over.

Tatterdemalion
Bride

TWO OF THE GUESTS ARE wearing the same hat. That is not to say that one straw boater, sprouting orange felt begonias from a green velvet ribbon, rests upon two heads connected at the chin of Siamese twins. Rather, that the great aunt—bride's party—and the godmother—groom's —are seated on either side of the aisle in the second row of pews, glaring at each other. Neither is willing to acquiesce to the law of the fashion *faux pas* that dictates: "She who arrives second must surrender." As they have both just noticed each other, the order of their arrival is disputable. Their silent duel goes unnoticed by the rest of the guests because their hats have disappeared in the symmetry of Mrs. Wimple's flower arrangements.

Mrs. Wimple plods around in rubber-soled sandals, plastic spray bottle in hand, squirting water on her posies to keep them looking as fresh for the last two weddings of the day as they did for the first two. The great-aunt and the godmother both get squirted, not because Mrs. Wimple is senile or near-sighted, but because she has noticed the identical hats and their symmetrical positions, and she just can't help herself. She has arranged flowers for the last 12,000 weddings in the church—four a day, two days a week, for the last twenty-eight-and-a-half years—and is amused by the obstinacy of the old gals. She wants to help move matters along, help the gals save face, by forcing one of them to remove the water-sodden felt and straw.

Another way would be to go outside and send a stone crashing through the stained-glass window that holds the image of Mary Magdalene. This would let in a strong wind that might blow off at least one of the hats, constituting an act of God. Of course, she wouldn't really do anything so disruptive. She's a little ashamed of herself for letting those thoughts shoot up to the surface. What if Father Herman were to catch wind of such impiety? Sometimes when he looks towards her from the altar, she is convinced that he can see the running playlet dancing behind her eyes. They are both naked, and he chases her around the pews, screaming, "Lorraine, Lorraine," and tearing fistfuls of flowers from her arrangements to press between their grinding loins. A swirl of fragrant, pink mist rises, mingling with their sweat, sanctifying their forbidden lust. Mrs. Wimple lowers her eyes as she squirts the flowers by the altar.

The groom is chatting with his younger brother, who is sitting in the front row. They are waving their hands at each other in gestures that translate into intercourse and masturbation. The groom is stone drunk and has momentarily forgotten all about the bride, or that he's about to get hitched. As he shakes the can of whipped cream, the hooker from the night before materializes in his alcoholic haze. She sashays down the aisle towards the altar, one long, blue, star-spangled nail tapping the clasp of her black, sequined g-string. The groom's hips thrust out towards her as his brother's high-pitched laugh shoots her between the eyes. She falls back and dissolves into the leftover confetti from the previous nuptials.

The younger brother's face glistens with excitement and envy. His spit-slicked hair falls into his eyes as he pictures his new sister-in-law naked and his older brother riding her like a cowboy. She has long, hanging breasts pierced with nipple rings. He only has *National Geographic* to go on. He doesn't even remotely expect the slap to the back of his head that his mother dispatches, having suddenly turned her attention away from the wardrobe of the bride's family to the hand signals of her sons.

The groom's mother curses her dead husband under her breath, then quickly crosses herself to reverse the sin. If he were alive, she'd be dressed in rose-coloured silk with sandals to match, instead of pea-green Dacron and her funeral shoes. Her boys would have manners and respect. The older one would not be getting sucked into that family of vipers. They didn't even have the manners to consult her on the wedding cake or the wine. Her barrel of red is the envy of the block. Even women with big-footed husbands do not have wine as tasty or clear as hers. Her son is no grand prize, but that bride is a conniving slut. That hair. Those shoes. Threw herself at the poor boy and look where he is now. She smoothes out the Dacron and peeks at the bride's mother's white shoes. She smugly studies a scuff mark near the toe. If her husband were alive, she'd be a real lady, not like that scuffed-up phony with her duck dishes filled with canned soup and processed cheese. She'd like to break those ducks over her head, one by one. She crosses herself again and smiles sweetly towards the bride's mother, then turns back to her sons. She raises a hand to slap the older one, but is stopped midway by red-faced Father Herman, in whose church it is taboo to smite the bride or groom before their big moment, no matter how sacriligiously either one is behaving.

Father Herman slowly runs his finger over his ornate robe and shivers. Its golden threads cast the fall of Lucifer, Sodom, and Gomorrah, and the stoning of whores, onto the faces of the guests. Father Herman is no stranger to masturbatory hand signals. He retaliates at the impropriety of the subject matter in his church by swinging the incense burner a little too close to the groom's head so that the holy smoke singes his ear.

The bride's mother is oblivious to all this because she is sifting through her white satin cocktail bag: lighter, cigarillos, coin purse, tissue for the requisite tears, and handgun. She cannot find the speech she has written for the reception; the words she so carefully chose to hide her disdain for the groom and his clan. Don't get her wrong; she also feels a fundamental relief that her snarling polecat of a daughter will soon be someone else's problem. But then, of course, there is Christmas dinner to worry about. She'll have to invite them and they're sure to make her drink more of that homemade, screw-top poison that they brought for the first meeting of the families. They had already broken not one, but two pieces of her goose-motif fine china—finger bowl and butter dish—with their thick hands. And they thought that money would reverse the transgression, the heathens. Of course, she couldn't accept. Don't be silly, what's a few broken dishes between families? Out of politeness she drank their wine while trying not to picture purple feet stomping through her mouth. The next morning broken china shards rattled in her head with every step.

She suddenly remembers. The speech is at home on the kitchen table, next to the inventory list of her china pattern with its thick, black lines crossing out the missing pieces. She notices the groom's mother smiling at her and she smiles back.

The bride's third cousin in the fourth row doesn't notice her aunt's spastic purse inventory because she's too busy making moony eyes and waving her pinkie in greeting at the date of the groom's second cousin in the third row across the aisle. She has not seen the bride for ten years and RSVP'd at the last minute out of boredom. She adjusts the neckline of her flowered frock to expose freckled cleavage and a hint of mauve, satin bra. She doesn't recognize anyone on her side of the church, not even her aunt. Were it not for the labelled guest book and donation box at the door, both decorated with kissing doves tied together by a white ribbon—the same doves that appeared on the wedding invitation—she could be at anyone's wedding. When she slit open the invitation, she imagined strangling the doves with the ribbon and the kind of sound they would make.

A hastily wrapped fondue set from her Christmas give-away closet sits on her lap. She fingers the hem of her dress, then slowly inches it up her thigh. She figures she's been invited to be an extra body in the church because she hasn't heard a peep from these people since the cancelled family reunion her aunt tried to organize five years earlier. Lack of enthusiasm, her aunt had said. As she winks and licks her upper lip with the tip of her tongue in the direction of the second cousin's date, she wonders what type of meat will be served at the reception.

The groom's second cousin does not notice the bride's third cousin devouring her date. She is trying to exude dignity by keeping her chin up and her gaze straight ahead to appease her own insecurity and shame in having rented a date for this occasion. She has paid for his suit, her corsage, and their cab fare. She'd had a hard enough time explaining to her female lover, yet again, that she could not come to the party. Her family was already whispering and signalling with their eyes whenever she walked into a room alone. Her lover stomped out of the house when the rented man appeared on their doorstep this morning. The second cousin chased her down the walkway in nylon-stockinged feet, begging and apologizing. She promised that next time they would both go, no matter what, and she'd even stick her tongue in her lover's ear in front of all of them. Small stones ripped holes in her reinforced toes as she chased, which accounts for the clash of Cinnamon Surprise hose with her aquamarine ensemble.

She fidgets in her seat, having now noticed the manoeuvres of the third cousin in the fourth row, and slips a small section of her date's skin between her nails, then squeezes and twists. He cringes and lets out a small cry, then guiltily faces the front of the church. If she has to hire men, they're damn well going to do the job right for her money.

The bride's father looks through the church doors at the backs of the guests' heads. He nods as he tallies each guest's weight, and then recalculates what each one is costing him in food and booze for the reception. Good thing he only ordered chicken. Damn his wife for producing a gaggle of daughters. This one isn't even his favourite and has given him more grief than the others combined with her weird hair and whore heels. The big toe on his left foot still hurts when it rains. She stabbed it with her heel, while blowing cigarette smoke in his face, when he wouldn't give her money for a tattoo of a penis. So she could do the fucking for a change, she'd said. She got the tattoo anyway by selling his vintage porn magazines to Boy Scouts for ten bucks a piece. He wondered if the Scouts told their parents why they wanted the cash. He once saw the black penis rising from her clean-shaven pussy. He couldn't resist. She caught him looking through the bathroom window and pulled open her lips and flashed him.

He jams his hands deep into the pockets of the rented pants that are chaffing his thighs and feels the familiar throbbing. He has lost his place, and starts over, counting heads, calculating weight while appeasing himself with the thought that after this she'll be gone, and he'll be safe.

The bride is in a small, dusty dressing room above the church, taking scissors to her dress. She knows exactly what's going on downstairs. She's glad she's alone. She has refused help from those clucking women with hat pins pinching their skulls. She doesn't know what has talked her into this wedding except for brainwashing from Cinderella and Snow White. Even her green hair hasn't completely bleached them out of her imagination. Or maybe it happened when her youngest sister cracked open her cow bank and spent her dollar coins on a pair of white lace, fingerless gloves with sewn-in pearls and star-shaped rhinestones. While the whole family screamed at the bride and cursed the day she was born, her little sister left the gloves under her pillow with a note that said, "So you can be a princess." She has never shown her little sister the penis. She wonders if it disqualifies her.

Pieces of fabric fall to the floor, crooked lace circles, taffeta crescents. The dress still feels too tight, and she manages to hack out the final piece as the music calls. She picks up her bouquet of wilted lilies and spits on it. She carefully steps into her stilettos.

The guests are on their feet and are staring anxiously at the tall wooden doors. The bride's little sister is prancing up and down the aisle, twirling her bluebell skirt and showering everyone with rose petals. She can't wait to see her sister. She knows she'll be more beautiful than Cinderella, Sleeping Beauty, and Snow White put together. The sound of breaking glass is heard, and a strong wind hurls the tall, wooden doors open, snatching the hats off the great aunt and the godmother and reducing Mrs. Wimple into fits of giggles. She tears a fistful of flowers from the last pew and stuffs them down her skirt. Father Herman throws her a dirty look, and she clams up, goes to the corner, and shuts her eyes. The groom goes sober and his jaw drops. He stares dumbly and scratches his crotch. The bride's mother lies motionless under the pew, her skirt twisted up over her hips, exposing her beige girdle. The guests grab their coats and gifts and stomp out past the bride, jeering at her and showing their teeth. They step over the bride's father who lies unconscious in the hallway amidst shards of stained glass. Through the hole in Mary Magdelene's stomach the next wedding party is seen turning tail, hitching up its skirts, and squealing its tires. In the hurly-burly, the third cousin pinches the butt of the second cousin's date and slips him her phone number. He winks and fondles her earring. The second cousin takes off her shoes and stands on the pew in awe. With one hand, Father Herman is banging his shoe on the altar and calling for order, while alternately praying for salvation and banishing demons without ungluing his eyes from the bride. His other hand is out of sight. Only the bride's little sister claps and squeals with glee because the bride is wearing her gloves.

What whips the beloved as the doors burst open is a swollen, naked belly, two dark brown nipples the size of dollar coins on breasts heavy with milk, and a black penis decorated with two kissing doves and a white ribbon, all framed by a trail of white lace and taffeta clouds.

SWAN DIVE

I can fly
I can fly
You can see my wings.
I fly in the breeze.

I. The cat disappeared.
AN ASSEMBLY LINE OF STRANGERS, friends, and relatives move a steady stream of cardboard boxes out of the building and into the truck. Actually, it is only a small blue van; mine was a compact life. Ashes to ashes, box upon box, my belongings are being stacked on each other's heads like the bones of the poor in a crowded mausoleum awaiting rebirth into another life in a new city.

But all is not well, despite the light-headed grin of my cousin, whose station in this assembly line is the lawn, and who is supposed to be making sure that grave robbers leave the contents of the tomb intact. I will need every artifact from my old life for my new one: books, Christmas decorations, scraps of paper that used to be stuck to the refrigerator—everything except my bags of spice.

Earlier that day, when I, the nearly-departed, was shoving

39

the last of my worldly possessions into a box that once housed sardines from Portugal, I spontaneously decided that I could not bear to pack one more thing. The bags of spice, I decreed, would be inherited by the fat woman who would be taking my place. Perhaps I had a premonition that spice would be unwelcome in the afterworld, that blandness would rule, that everything would lose its taste. Maybe that's why the cat, in those last moments, disappeared.

How do you leave a well-devised, though stagnating, life with its familiar streets you can bike down with your eyes closed, its old comfortable lovers and its prospective lovers you've saved for a rainy day, its accepted problems that you don't even lose sleep over anymore, and its reliable Saturday night distractions? You dive, thumb and forefinger squeezing nostrils, eyelids glued shut, air stored in puffed out cheeks. You just jump and hope to land somewhere soft so the majority of important bones will be left intact.

As I stand on the roof of the four-story brownstone, I look down at the gathering crowd and resort to some last minute meditation, breathing, chanting, "I am not crazy; all will be well. I am not crazy; all will be well." My target is the blue van parked in front of the building. The paint is smooth. There is no wind. This is a good sign.

Surveying my life one last time, I spot my cousin still sitting on the lawn, now bereft of my possessions, still smiling at strangers. What is she smiling about? This is not a happy occasion. Ignorance must be bliss.

And there is my lover, the artist, in his checkered shirt and rumpled green work pants. I'm not sure if he looks cheerful or wistful. Whatever the look, it is frozen on his face. Just like when I told him, in passing, that I was planning to move on. Normally, I wouldn't consult anyone on a matter this personal, but I'd been fucking him for a year and thought he might notice I was gone. Of course, he'd always have the slides. Those cold, calculated images of naked people in compromising positions that are the basis of his drawings. Captives, surrendering their bodies to his fantasies, willingly trading their souls to the artist for a taste of immortality. Fools.

The first time he and I were alone together, I shed my clothes slowly. Shirt first, black bra and jean skirt remaining.

Directions: Pretend you're sitting at a table talking to someone. Strike a natural pose. No, that doesn't look right; stick your elbow out more. Good. Snap.

All his suggested positions were very unnatural.

It's hard to play in someone else's playground, half-clothed, without laughing. But don't laugh; the bestower of immortality did not choose you for your sense of humour. Because you are tall and angular, you will be transformed into his Queen of Angst.

Directions: Maybe the bra should come off now. That's right, walk around to the other side of the imaginary table and lean on your elbow. Look at your invisible cohort as if you are trying to understand.

Trying to understand what? Why I was topless and having a conversation with someone who wasn't there? Or why I sometimes caught him looking at my breasts as if they were forbidden golden apples that he wanted to bite into without consequence?

He continued to instruct me on clothes removal, but now it had the rhythm of a slow striptease, his eyes dancing over the curves of my body. Stark naked on the cold floor, I pretended to hold up a crumbling ceiling. He ordered me to look desperate, and I tried, but when he wasn't looking I'd snigger, or grin, or giggle. The camera noticed, and the artist frowned, told me that angst would not be possible with my silly face. A thousand pardons, artist sir, but walls crumbling around me was just too unnatural a pose. What was I to imagine? That I'd stepped out of the shower just as the upstairs neighbour's toilet, which had been leaking for a month, was about to come crashing through my ceiling unless I could hold it up with all my might?

Maybe that's not what he had in mind. But I know now that he could not have pulled off that image of me, even if I'd given him my best anguished face, because I, or at least my breasts, had captured him, had drawn him into his own image. He could no longer cast me as a despairing, solitary woman trapped in a stark world crumbling down around her because he could never visit that world. He'd be too scared. It might not be fun and mean things might be said. He might have to deal with dirty dishes, cold drafts, and PMS.

Once, while massaging my legs, he told me he wanted to mold my thigh into a different shape, and worked at it diligently, intensely for over an hour before accepting that I wasn't made of clay.

When sex between us was still hypothetical, he would question me about positions and angles I preferred, looming above me, anxiously awaiting instruction. With the crazed, happy face of a mad scientist, he'd bend my limbs accordingly. He would then close his eyes, laugh out loud, and clap his hands, as if he'd stolen something and had gotten away. He needed the picture in his mind to place himself in the art. My inner ear could hear him counting off the shots when we finally did connect. Position one, leg over shoulder. *Snap.* Position two, lips to clitoris. *Snap.* Position three, orgasm. Smile. *Snap.* Did you enjoy that, Thalia?

At the vernissage, I followed posters of my golden apples up the stairs into the gallery. As I perused the artist's charcoal manipulations, I was seized by a despairing, solitary angst. I did not see myself anywhere, which was sort of a good thing because my likeness appeared unclothed in situations with people I'd never consider taking my clothes off for. It was as if I'd suddenly discovered that I was afflicted with a multiple personality disorder because two of my personalities had shown up at the same time—the one on the floor, sipping bad white wine, suddenly shocked by the appearance of the other one, naked, on the wall. As I examined my double's body for the mark of the devil, I heard whispering behind me. Two men were staring and pointing at me and the drawing. My arms involuntarily folded over my chest, and I slunk towards the bar to sort myself out.

A crowd was gathered around what was to be the portrait of angst. The canvas was huge. I was almost life-sized, and my breasts were shining beacons calling people towards the drawing. But there were no crumbling walls around me, and no look of fear on my face. The artist had turned me into a wood nymph. And I was not alone. Both my personalities looked rather surprised. There was a man with an erect penis squatting down beside me. We were in the enchanted garden of the Hesperides, the only place to find forbidden golden apples, and my outstretched hands were searching through a ceiling of branches. He was rummaging through twigs and pebbles at my feet, while looking into my pubic hair, that dark patch which the artist had worked on extra hard to make aesthetic, appealing, and well-groomed. He proudly pointed out his achievement to his audience. At first glance, I thought the squatting, erect elf was the artist himself: a happy, horny sprite waiting to taste the fruit of his labours—as soon as the pesky onlookers went away. This garden was a place the artist could visit, a land where no one did anything but play quietly in the branches. But upon closer inspection of the drawing, it wasn't the artist at all, but his younger brother—an easy compromise between his desire to be there and his strange need to remain uninvolved.

His brother stood by me while I studied the drawing, his forearm skimming mine. From the look on his face, I could tell that in the next scene in his imagination he and I were rolling around on the branches, making love. From behind a distant stump, the fully-clothed artist watched with glee. I, on the other hand, imagined my hand poking through the branches and inadvertently knocking on the door of a hornet's nest. The stingers swarm the garden, and both figures run out of the drawing to look for their clothes. They never go back to that garden, preferring the safety of four walls, mosquito netting, and the comfort of a queen-sized bed. They date for a while, catch the occasional movie, maybe a concert, and they talk on the phone, trying to figure out each other's insides. But the artist would never want to be implicated in anything so mundane.

The drawing was the first to sell to someone seduced by the artist's vision. On some days, his vision even suited me. Then again, the artist would never actually let me move into his garden. I might want to put on some clothes and pull up some weeds. I'd want to speak. I wasn't really even in the drawing.

In a movie of my life, the definitive scene the next day would look like this:

SCENE 34. THE BIG QUESTION. DAY.
"I need to know what you want out of this relationship before I make my decision." Thalia plays guitar on a strand of hair she's plucked from her head. From the other side of the table,

silence, clench-toothed grin, quick ingestion of salad leaf, quick chewing. Does she like the way he chews enough to stay?

"If you want me to stay, I might." He is kind of cute, in a goofy sort of way. Her hand slides across the table to touch his, but he pulls his hands away and hides them between his thighs. He keeps eating, dropping his face into his paper plate, picking up choice morsels with his teeth. Inhaling of cherry tomato, dribble of tomato juice on lower lip, more silence.

Thalia loses her appetite at the exact moment when she would like to at least be able to start eating, just to have something to do in the silence. Instead, she picks up a bread stick and starts fencing. She taunts the salt shaker.
CUT.

In the final weeks, the artist became my dream lover. Charming, imaginative, altruistic, enthusiastic, attentive, even a little sad. Suddenly sad. Imagine that. He moped around my apartment like an abandoned dog, occasionally peeing on a cardboard box. I turned to tarot cards, crystal balls, and dreams to try and extract meaning from his sudden sadness, but no sign came.

We saw each other every day, slept together every night. We made love for hours, like desperate people who know death is near. We missed appointments, phone calls, the passing time.

And then came the last weekend. The artist delivered pink carnations to make up for his absence and then left town. How unimaginative, how unenthusiastic, how inattentive, how selfish. I tried to make love to the flowers, but when I kissed them, they tasted like lye soap, and when I pressed them between my thighs, they fell apart.

I toss the crushed carnations at the cheering crowd, take a deep breath, the last lung-full of air from this spot, in this life, close my eyes so tightly that blue spots appear, guiding me towards the blue van, lean out over the edge—and stop. My survey missed my cat. Where is my cat? I can't go anywhere without my cat.

II. The artist cried.
What do you do when you know your number's up, but you're afraid to turn in your ticket because even a half-baked life is better than nothing? You make a plan. A plan so exact, so carved in stone, or at least in your bank account, that there's no backing out of it. You embarrass yourself into doing whatever you think it is you should do by telling everyone you know that you are doing it. You argue with them over the pros and cons. Assure them that you're a much bigger and better human being than all those people who tried and failed before you. Tell them that if they have nothing positive to say, they should just shut up.

After declaring yourself immense and beyond repercussion, should you secretly, deep in your gut, in nightmares of falling off cliffs and into the mouths of multi-headed beasts, change your mind, you're stuck, sister. You see, you've built a framework of expectations that you can no longer escape. A personal tower of Babel, crookedly raised by your inner braggart and by the voices of admiring friends who are waiting for you to dive off the top and survive.

Naturally, there are those who will try to keep you from jumping. Who send out psychic lassos to rope your wander-lusting spirit, your adventuresome soul. There is one person in particular so imbued with power that while I am on the edge of the roof, surveying my life, noticing the absence of my cat, she is shooting death rays out of her eyes that throw me back.

I try to ignore her, but I can't, never could, no matter how big the crowd was, and no matter how far back she was sitting, beaming at my rendition of the Gingerbread Boy song. I stood there in my purple velvet and white lace dress, unable to hide. She didn't realize while she was sitting there, touting my accomplishments to Mr. and Mrs. Lentil, that I was the only child on the entire stage who had forgotten the paper gingerbread boy prop I'd worked on all week for this grand finalé. The prop that was way more fun to make than learning the entire gingerbread boy story by heart so I could be the narrator in a purple velvet and white lace dress instead of something neat, like the dancing bowl of icing. And while all the other children were singing the annoying little song at the top of their screechy, little lungs, *I'm the gingerbread boy I am, I am, the gingerbread boy am I . . .* , I was turning a deep shade of magenta because not only had I left my prop at the podium, the loss of the prop had perturbed me so much I'd lost all the words to the song and I was waving an empty hand around stupidly, moving my lips randomly, pretending to be singing. I was sure the entire audience had noticed my blunder because Mary-Beth Lentil next to me had and glared at me through the whole song, bulgy-eyed and pinch-lipped. And through all of this confusion and embarrassment, hard as I tried, I could still see the gleam of that motherly smile, that overbearing, expectant pride that would redeem her life. It tickled me under the chin and bathed me in mother-love light so bright that anyone who hadn't noticed I was not singing and I had no damned gingerbread boy to wave around surely would with the neon aura surrounding me. What was even worse was that Mom might notice and would trade me in for a less defective child.

In later life, I tried not to invite Mom to my big moments.

Mom. Standing among the crowd. Trying to will me away from the edge. Trying to break into the blue van, drive it to her house, where she can shove my worldly possessions into what used to be my room and is now a shrine: princess furniture, stuffed bear, gorilla, mouse, and rainbow comforter all exactly as I left them. Mom, who tries to shrink me so she can remain young and beautiful, the talk of the neighbourhood. "She's too young to be your mother, she must be your sister." Mom glows, I cry. Little kids need to know who Mom is. Mom, whose words of feigned concern have added the final rung to the ladder, have unknowingly become one with the wind that will push me off the roof.

SCENE 25. THE BIG BID. AFTERNOON.

"Now you're sure you want to do this, sweetie? It's not too late to change your mind."

Thalia presses her nose to the car window and stares at what used to be the open fields of her childhood but is now a new neighbourhood, complete with copycat box houses and street names that must have been hasty decisions.

"You should be around people who love you, your family."

Thalia fiddles with the car radio, goes through all the stations three times, turns the radio off. She looks through her purse for nothing in particular.

"What I mean is that you're a creative person and this is your home. I'm sure you can manage here if you really try. And you can always move in with me if that will make it easier."

Mom turns to Thalia and smiles, a pathetic, needy smile. A smile that pleads with Thalia to stay because she's her only friend left in the whole world. To stay for her sake because she has run out of people to listen to her gripe about her long lost men, her health, her decomposing life, since she has kicked out, alienated, or been abandoned by just about everybody else. Tragic figure with her long red hair, faded jeans and sneakers, driving a Japanese import. An attractive body hiding a quickly rusting interior.

Thalia finds an old piece of bubble gum at the bottom of her purse, peels off the wrapper, and pops the gum into her mouth. It is hard and takes extra effort to chew. As she blows slow, purple bubbles, Mom nearly sideswipes a van brimming with teenage boys. First they swear at her, then they wolf-whistle. She is momentarily distracted from her mission. *CUT.*

In those final weeks, Mom tried her best to figure out what my requirements for friendship were, something she'd had no clue about until now. First she tried calling me everyday, "Just to chat." When she realized that even my answering machine wouldn't talk to her anymore, she staggered her calls to every third day. The artist and I, usually in bed, would wager on how many times she would let the phone ring.

But like the revelation of the moth just before it shrivels in the flame, a light must have suddenly flicked on in Mom's head. She stopped chain-smoking in my tiny apartment so I didn't have to drag everything I owned out onto the fire escape after she left. She befriended my cat and pet it lovingly without rolling her eyes. She didn't even pick off his stray hairs from her clothes, not in front of me, anyway. In mixed company, stories that started, "Remember when you were five, Thalia, and you peed your pants in the stuck elevator . . ." did not tumble from her lips no matter how much wine she'd sipped, or how little the conversation revolved around her. When I would finally answer the phone, there were no incriminatory silences, and she'd have a plan, an actual plan: a foreign film, including location, time, director, and plotline; the latest play that was not a musical; a gallery where '70s counter-culture art was on display, "because I know how much you liked that Pistol group." If I politely declined, she'd graciously accept. Just like that. No arguments. No allegations of selfishness or lack of love. No accusations that I preferred the company of my friends over hers. No slamming the phone in my ear, then calling back to slam the phone in my ear again.

She stopped harping about my move and sent some of my stuffed animals to needy children in Guatemala. Without taking credit for my courage ("I'm not just saying it because she's flesh of my flesh . . . "), she told people I'd make it wherever I went, and she was proud that I wasn't afraid to take the leap. A bilious uncle, who insisted I was doomed to the drug-in-the-drink fate, and would be ruined as soon as I left the extended family web, had his throat sliced by her tongue, and was never heard from again.

She even did her best to stifle her favourite motherly admonition: "Now you know I'm against it, honey, but I want you to make you own decision." Even when my plan was to sell antiperspirant stones door to door, or to wear a long black wig and a clip-on earring in my nose and sell false fortunes to the gullible. I was testing her.

In those final weeks, I actually started to like her as a full-fledged person, instead of seeing her as lumbering Mom. She was making an effort to understand me and what I wanted, separate from her—a fresh start, a bigger pond. It was as if she had finally bought the dictionary necessary to understand my foreign tongue. I began to realize that she was just another Jane who did what she could, while she could, and had made some mistakes. She had bravely moved from husband to husband, country to country while always remembering that my feet were growing and that I'd need new shoes. She'd had me young, by accident. But she never regretted, never looked back. Wasn't she a bit like me?

Looking down into the crowd, I try to make eye contact with Mom. I blow her bubble-gum kisses and wave, but she's not looking my way. I'm your friend, Jane. Look up, look way up. I smile and wave both my hands in the air like a stranded motorist. The crowd thinks it's aerobics and follows my lead. All except Jane, who is preoccupied. I'm still going to go, Jane, as soon as I find my cat, but why don't you come visit sometime, and we'll pick it up from here. Long distance relationships do have their benefits. My hands rest upon my hipbones. Why isn't she looking back up at me? She's going to miss my triple-loop swan dive, my big moment. You're going to miss my big moment, Jane.

Jane is deep in conversation with the artist, my artist. He looks perturbed, and his face is falling to the pavement. The artist is crying. Great, now he cries.

I throw a pebble at Jane to get her attention. The pebble misses her and hits the windshield of the Japanese import. She swings around and squints up at me. It's hard to tell whether she is angry or happy, but her look smacks me on the forehead, keeling me over onto the roof. It takes a few seconds for the grey mist to lift from my eyes. As it does, I see her in another light. And I can see inside her car, too. Isn't that my cat with its nose pressed against the window?

III. It hailed rotten fruit.
Life turns into art because of boredom. You lock yourself into a role, play the part with complete integrity, and wait for the

applause. No situation runs its own course. Everything is preplanned, controlled, from prologue through plot, to self-fulfilling denouément. If you are consistent enough, other people will establish roles for themselves around you: the reluctant lover afraid of the dark; the aging mother trying to stop time; the needy friends begging drinks from your well. You play off each other with seasoned grace, repeating well-worn scenes with slight variation so you can pretend you are doing something new. Do engineers see life as a blueprint with a foundation and supports holding up the entire structure? Do doctors see it as a disease to be diagnosed, cured, or let run its course? Do seamstresses cut out a pattern and then nip, tuck, and hem as things go in and out of style? Was my life to continue as a theme with variations, a *leitmotif* in a low-budget art film?

The film crew has arrived, and a dozen lackeys are busily sweeping the sidewalk in front of the brownstone, carefully strewing garbage and dead leaves in other areas to specification. Torches are being screwed into the lawn. They're going for a primal, ritualistic, though urban feel for this final scene. The director is rearranging people's chosen positions. To my dismay, the artist and Jane are brought closer together. The smiling cousin is moved off the lawn to make room for more torches and is told to squat upon a yellow, marble bowling ball so she looks like a content hen. Make-up artists are quickly painting frowns on some people, touching up other's smiles. Extras are being bussed in, strangers who are given specific instructions: laugh out loud, roll your eyes, point, and chant, "Jump, bitch, jump." One extra looks like a bum, and none of the others want to stand next to him. A lackey is dispatched to fumigate him with cheap perfume. The bum's task is to laugh out loud, as if he knows something I don't, some secret that's hidden in the tatters of his filthy brown coat. He practices his laugh between taking swigs from a mickey when he thinks no one is looking. When he sees I'm watching, he gives me the finger.

Lights are being set up to illuminate the roof from below. Another lackey is polishing the van with a toothbrush, and I wonder about the nature of his crime. The director is shouting something up at me through a megaphone that I don't understand, but makes everyone on the ground, including the bum and my imbecile cousin, laugh.

The director is a woman dedicated to her work. She knows what she wants and how to get it out of people. She's like a whip-master, flogging our little lives into shape. Some people trust her savvy completely, while others have taken me aside to complain that their major talents were ignored when scripts were being handed out at the door. A few have tried to get me to use my influence with her to improve their lot. But I have no influence. I auditioned like everyone else.

The role I'd prepared for didn't seem bad. The character was attractive and quirky. She was loved and needed by many. Well-travelled, well-spoken, and talented, she was a good person to invite to parties because she sang opera when she got drunk. She had good judgment, an analytical mind, and the impetuousness to get what she wanted most of the time. She was the lead. I could be her, no problem.

The director sat next to me in the dark screening room; she had called me back to watch my audition, to point out my deficiencies. I had never seen myself in motion before. I didn't want to see myself as others saw me because I was afraid I wouldn't measure up to what I'd set out to be, that I'd see a half-assed imitation of my imagined self, not even close to the lofty heights of my pretensions. Or even worse, I'd see the part of me that I carefully shackled to my bed each morning—the part that stumbled over words and non-existent stones when people were watching too closely.

Numbers on the screen counted down to the sudden appearance of my face in extreme close-up. I could see the anxiety huddled in the whites of my eyes, and I buried my face in my hands against my own fear. But I peeked through my fingers as the camera pulled back. Re-live and learn.

I am sitting alone on an empty set. My heart is pounding in my head, and my hands are clammy. There are sweat prints where I have been clutching the script, wringing it like a wet rag. I dab my forehead with it to keep from passing out. I want the role so badly I can taste it. It tastes like a mouthful of fresh melon and vodka. It slides down my throat, both cooling and burning my insides. A bright light is blinding me, and I strain to see the director, but she is invisible in the dark. Her voice commands me as if it were inside my head.

"Have you read the whole script, Miss?"

I nod once, not able to make a sound.

"Do you understand this character and her role in the story?"

I nod again, exhibiting the enthusiasm of a circus horse. I almost stick my tongue out for a lump of sugar.

"I have chosen a scene from Thalia's life that I consider crucial. Mary Beth, the script girl, will assist you. Please begin on page 125."

I whinny.

I have memorized the entire script backwards and forwards. I flip through the pages in my mind, eager to demonstrate how well I understand the role, how effortless it is for me to play it. I stop on page 125, and freeze. I haven't worked on this scene. It scared me and I'd hoped to postpone it. I didn't think it would come up so soon. Please don't let me blow it, I pray to the deities. I'm not up for any other roles. This is the only one I've learned.

SCENE 48. THE BIG LEAP. NIGHT.
Thalia removes her clothing: first her shoes and socks, then her long black dress. She fumbles with the buttons down the back, a childish tactic to delay the inevitable. Defrocked, she turns her back to the camera and climbs onto the wooden chair. Her toes grope against the chair's grain as she inches towards the edge of the seat. She pushes up on her toes and the back legs of the chair lift off the floor, almost throwing her over. Regaining her balance, she begins again, her heart thumping in the hollowness of her chest.

"Take off the bra," a disembodied voice directs, and though this is not in the script, Thalia reaches between her breasts and sets them free.

She closes her eyes and creates the audience in her mind, the curious and anxious faces of the strangers, friends, and relatives who have gathered to witness her final flight. Her hips begin to sway back and forth to a rhythm controlled by her heartbeat. She takes a deep breath and stretches her arms out towards her sides. She resembles a butterfly pinned to black velvet. She hears footsteps, and two figures approach her from the sidelines. She squints through the blackness, but can only make out shapes. The figures kneel on either side of the chair simultaneously, as if they were mirror images, and plant their dry lips on her ankles. Thalia suppresses her urge to giggle as their tongues trace her anklebones, then slide up her legs like snails.

The white light shining down on her from above burns her skin with its intensity, and a drop of sweat trickles down her forehead towards the tip of her nose, where it hangs like a jewel before falling to its death. Thalia hears it splash onto the floor far below. Her arms and legs begin to stiffen as she stands there, motionless, and she cannot feel the nips the shadowy figures take from her fingertips or the sharpness of their teeth against the inside of her wrists. It is only when the flesh breaks that a sharp ache travels up her arms. She squeezes her eyes tighter, trying to suppress the pain.

Thalia tries to speak her lines, but no words form on her tongue, in her brain, as if her body has been cut off from its logic. A cloud of grey dots appears before her eyes, and she feels her senses shutting down, one at a time. Just before her vision snuffs out, she looks towards the figures one final time; she can see them now, as if she's gained second sight. They are glowing red in the dark, filled with her essence.

The lines are fed to her by the script girl and Thalia opens her mouth and delivers them, though she is unable to hear what she's saying. The words tumble out, atonal and shrill as screeching brakes. She is unable to control their rhythm, despite her swaying hips. She screams, then whispers, then screams again.

"Drink up, dear friends, strangers, relatives, I have blood enough for everyone . . ."
CUT.

But the camera didn't stop recording. The director cringed and half-covered her eyes as the scene continued, and I shrunk in my seat until my feet couldn't touch the floor.

The figures move away from me. Either my voice has scared them off or they've had their fill. They twirl towards the sidelines like red lights, then expire. I raise my arms straight above my head, and the shadow of wings spans out by my sides. Blood from my wounds runs down my arms, two red rivers moving slowly towards each other, joining and comingling between my pale breasts, then rushing down towards my belly and filling a red pool under the chair. The cameraman mercilessly focuses on my face. As I try to retrieve the next line, a furious heat rises from a volcano in my chest. It pounds and spews sharp bits of rock that pierce my brain, puncturing its reservoirs. Tears flood my cheeks as the explosions become more intense, rattling my body and throwing it gracelessly to the floor. My cheek lies next to the red pool, and my head is so heavy that I can't lift it to see the expression on the director's face, which is good because I'm really embarrassed. But I can see Mary Beth, the script girl, glaring at me from the sidelines.

I've lost it. My composure, the role, the next line. I am spread-eagled on the stage, weeping.

"Excuse me, Miss. Miss?" the director calls out impatiently.

I look like a turtle as I raise my head from the floor.

"That's very impressive, but that's not in the script. You're supposed to dive, not topple. Can you please stick to the script?"

Nodding weakly, I crawl back onto the chair and squeeze my wrists to extract more blood. I touch the raised skin around the small puncture marks, then bring my fingertips to my lips. The steely taste of my blood sends a jolt through my brain. Auto-electroshock. Suddenly I know this has gone too far.

I reach for my black dress, crumpled on the floor behind me, and retrieve a tissue from my pocket to stanch the bleeding. But the blood won't stop leaking. As one spring is plugged, a new one spurts on another part of my body. I start tearing the dress into strips and wrapping tourniquets around my limbs. My wounds are bleeding profusely and, as I tie the last strip of fabric around my throat, I begin to black out. My breathing is faint and strained, and I can hardly hear the director yelling at me to stay in character, and that the show must go on.

Someone yells *Action*, and red lights flood the roof. As I open my eyes, I see my friends, my cousin, my mother, the artist down on the ground. There are fresh carnations at my feet, and the crowd is applauding and chanting my name. I bow dizzily and back away from the edge, hypnotized by the sweet devotion of my fans. Storm clouds huddle overhead.

Entranced by their love, I float back to the edge for another bow and the crowd goes wild. How can I leave this life with all the applause, where I'm so vital to the artistry of so many people's lives? Maybe there's still time to change my mind.

I start tearing off my tourniquets and throwing the bloody strips ecstatically into the audience. They suck on the strips and howl as if I were the moon. My wounds start spurting blood again and, as I pose with outstretched arms to absorb their chants, I become a gothic fountain petrified on the edge of the roof, raining blood on everyone below. The lines now come to me as easily as if I'd made them up myself:

"Drink up, dear friends, strangers, relatives, I have blood enough for everyone. The well is bottomless. You have made me into the spring of life and, in return for immortality, I offer you my animal spirits. Drink, drink until my blood rises to your eyes. I will live within all of you, serve as your muse, your fountain of youth, and your immutable wailing wall." I bless and baptize them with my waving hands.

Having ripped off the final tourniquets, I stand there naked, completely drained of all desire. I begin to shiver. The dark clouds move in closer, and I lift my hands above my head to keep them from swallowing me. It takes some effort. The artist is crying tears of appreciation for my final artistic act. His work is done. I have finally become the woman of his nightmares. He can hold on to the image forever. He can derive years of inspiration from this moment, and I will no longer be around to spoil it with silly grins. *Snap.* He disappears in the blaze of the flash cube.

Jane is pointing at me, then at herself, as she gloats to the Lentils. She looks up, way up, and lassos me around the waist with a tangled beam of pride, expectation, and victory. She winds the other end of the rope around her own waist, tugs it, and I'm jostled forward. She turns it like a jump rope, and I dance through its revolutions like a frenzied puppet, trying not to trip. The audience cheers and she takes a bow. I bite through the rope and she falls. A young man helps her up and into her car. She drives off with him laughing. My insides ache. The low-hanging clouds spit on me.

The show must go on. I try a few steps of my own, but the audience stands stock-still, unimpressed. This is not what they came to see. A few people boo, some heckle. The director is signalling to the cameraman to stop shooting.

My arms wave clumsily above my head and I spin, pirouetting until I don't know which side of the roof I'm on. I have lost the script, and I move my lips hoping that the words will just come to me, but all that comes out is gibberish, like that of a newborn. I cannot move. My nakedness embarrasses me and I try to hide my breasts with my hands. I look for my clothes but find only rags, which I plaster to my wet body. I'm as cold as a bird that has flown through a hailstorm.

I start to feel weak and look down into the crowd for help. All I can see are hands raised towards me and hungry, open mouths. The blood has stopped flowing, and I press on my veins to squeeze out more, but none comes, only rain. The crowd starts to scatter, running for shelter. Some familiar faces are cursing me from under their jackets, tossing the tourniquet strips into the gutter. The paid help waits impatiently, raising red umbrellas, howling and stamping their feet.

I hear a crying noise behind me. My cat jumps into my arms, wet and frightened. He has either escaped my mother, or has been hiding behind the chimney all this time. At this point, it doesn't matter where he's been, I'm just glad he's back. He is carrying a small bag of cardamom in his teeth, and I pack some powder into my open wounds.

The crowd is throwing tin cans and dirty looks up at me, demanding more juice, more performance, more satisfaction. "Stay in character," the hecklers screech. Greedy, unimaginative bastards. The amorphous figures get into a cab and are whisked away. The director is banging on the door to the roof, screaming that I'll never work in this town again.

A can hits the chimney. It sounds like the last chime of a tin church bell. My cat sits on my shoulder and purrs. He sandpapers my wounds shut with his tongue, and his fur tickles my ear. It begins to hail rocks, glass, and rotten fruit. I fall to my knees and cover my head with my hands. My cat, underneath me, keeps my belly warm.

I hate this audience. I'm tired of this role, of being the lead. The director can be fired. Was jumping my idea or hers? I can't remember. It dawns on me that I can go back into my empty apartment and make up a new ending. Maybe I can start a new story altogether, with a devoted prince, a kindly queen, many faithful servants, and a dozen bowls of ripe fruit. This thought gives me the strength to stand up. In defiance, I lean over for one final bow and to show my incisors. My cat on my shoulder shows his, too.

A bolt of lightning pokes out of a low hanging cloud and stings me, propelling me off the edge. For a few seconds, I float freely above the crowd. I twist and somersault awkwardly through the air—the reluctant trapeze artist, still looking for a net. But slowly wings unfold at my sides. My ankles join gracefully and my back arches, as if I've done this a thousand times before. I smile and shut my eyes, letting the wind guide me. I dive through the top of the blue van. It is pitch dark, hollow and silent inside. I am afraid to breathe because of the echo.

SILENT LAMENT

A GREY DAY AT THE BUS STOP and no one talks. It is a thick, opaque grey that blurs the distinctions between early morning and dusk, melding the beginning and the end of the day into one colourless moment. The absence of conversation makes the wait eternal, the unsynchronized second hands of loud wristwatches prolonging the minutes threefold, pulling each of the waiting passengers deep into their own isolation.

Cinda is cold. Her feet are damp, and her toes are shrivelling inside her shoes. She leans up against a telephone pole and drums her fingers nervously on its uneven, rotten wood. Tiny splinters enter her fingertips with every hit, and she begins to drum quicker, embedding the slivers deeper into her flesh, feeling little pinpoints of pain spread throughout her hand and up into her forearm. At least she feels something. This is her first day out since John left, and the world has an unreal quality about it, like a bleak expressionist painting with all the characters' mouths painted out. Cinda parts her lips slightly, as if to release a whisper, but then brings them together again. She can think of nothing to say. She stares at the others at the stop, willing them to come to life, to say something, to catch her eye, but no one risks intimacy at almost eight a.m. She drives several layers of splinters into her fingertips for company.

A businessman in a turquoise trenchcoat huddles in the doorway of a closed-down shop. His fists are jammed into his coat pockets, and his bald spot is reddened by the onslaught of rain mixed with hail, the size and consistency of tiny ball bearings. Two even streams of condensation pour out of his over-wide nostrils as he mechanically checks his wrist-watch and then sighs impatiently. When the minute hand reaches the hour mark and the bus has not come, he leaves his perch and paces through the puddles on the sidewalk, like the Cartesian automata that stroll the faces of Swiss clocks every hour and bash each other's skulls with mallets.

He is actively unattractive. He picks unrepentantly at his bulbous nose, dark bags pull his bloodshot eyes onto his cheeks, and a small, uneven moustache creeps across his upper lip like a centipede. Cinda pictures herself walking up to him, slipping her splintered fingers into his shirt and squeezing his nipples—just to see if he'll cry out. Just to touch skin other than her own. She wraps her arm around the telephone pole to keep herself from doing anything drastic.

She fixes her gaze on a fifteen-year-old girl puffing on a long, slim cigarette. The girl scowls and poses, hand on hip. She believes this makes her look older. She has spent hours in front of her mirror perfecting her "fuck the world and die" look—abject boredom, impatient superiority and petulance, head cocked slightly to the side. This is in contrast to her long, blonde, braided hair, her smooth pink cheeks, and her girls' school tunic. She is sorely embarrassed when a choking fit disrupts her composure.

The girl is quite beautiful and fresh in a typical blonde, upturned-nose fashion. Cinda imagines the girl watching herself silently in her bedroom mirror late at night. Running her fingertips over her half-lemon breasts, down her flat belly and into the slickness between her legs. The fair hairs on her arms and nape stand erect as the girl pictures another hand, a boy's hand or her best girlfriend's, gliding down the same line, a hand buried up to the wrist inside her. Cinda moans quietly and her hand reaches out to stroke the girl's hair, but is caught in the act. The girl turns around and throws her a dirty look that snaps Cinda's hand back. She buries the hand into her own hair. She is shocked at herself. She wonders what John would say if he could see her so weak. He probably wouldn't say anything, but would stare at her dolefully. This thought makes her want to cry. Perhaps today was too soon.

The bus finally comes, splashing Cinda's ankles with gutter water. The businessman shoves his way to the front of the line, flashing his passcard to the driver and pushing through the crowd bunched up at the front of the bus. His briefcase grazes Cinda. The girl delicately snuffs out her cigarette on the telephone pole and then slips the butt behind her ear. The bus driver stops her at the fare box, demanding she pay full fare. She insists she's a student, and her grey pleated uniform provides ample proof, but the driver is determined to have his way, to stick to the rules, to turn someone's—anyone's—day into a nosebleed. Cinda is glad she's been spared.

Without a word, Cinda offers the girl a few coins then glares at the driver, trying to communicate that she knows he hates young pretty things because they always hated him. He probably grew those jowls when he was six. Cinda wonders what they would feel like kneaded between her palms. The driver ignores her. The girl refuses the change and stomps off the bus. She relights her cigarette and stares off into the horizon as if she's been wronged by her lover, but is trying to maintain her composure. Stupid girl, Cinda thinks. One day she'll learn that a bus ride in the rain is better than pathos on a wet sidewalk.

Cinda seats herself between an old lady in a hairnet and a sleeping construction worker. The old lady's nose whistles irregularly when she breathes. The sleeping man snorts into Cinda's ear, and his head lolls towards her shoulder. She is terrified of the contact, cheek to shoulder, and what might happen. His fly is half-open, and she can see the indentation of his curled, hard cock against his blue underwear. She can almost smell the musty sweat trapped between folds of skin, fermenting sex ready to burst out of his pants. She quickly moves to a vacated single seat and does not, for the first time, worry about having rejected her former neighbours.

She closes her eyes and slips into the indentation John's body left in her mattress, the gap that pulls her in the moment she falls asleep. It smells of him in there, and in the morning her nostrils are filled with his fading scent: bitter sweat and tobacco. After he left her, she opened all her windows so the sharp autumn air could flush him out, but his smell won't go away. It jumps out of books of poetry, cookie jars, and fresh linen. It seeps into her nostrils and up behind her eyes, changing how everything looks. Even on this bus, amid the lost lovers of strangers, she can still smell him, as if he's sitting on her shoulder. He whispers, "Be quiet," as he slips his hand down the front of her shirt before she can protest.

Cinda slides open the bus window and takes a deep breath. Tiny drops of rain sprinkle her shoulder and sleeve. She wonders momentarily if the other passengers are cold, but leaves the window open anyway.

The driver grumbles out street names and slams on the brakes unnecessarily, jostling everyone forward. Cinda looks at her watch and realizes she's going to be late. The funny thing is, she doesn't even care. She slips her hand into her coat and squeezes her left breast to shut it up.

A little girl with carrot hair and a large toffee-coloured mole on her cheek gets on the bus, pulling her bag-laden mother towards the last seat. She twists the hem of her dress around her finger and, in a high-pitched voice, yaks excitedly at a frenzied pace, as if all the words she knows must be rattled off at regular intervals or she will forget them. They will leave her, feeling useless and neglected, never to come back.

Save your words, Cinda wants to warn her. Start saving now, because one day you'll need them to mean something and they'll be meaningless, drained, irrelevant. She reaches out to touch the little girl's arm, but the girl's mother yanks her daughter out of Cinda's grasp.

John's silence still hovers over her bed like a leaden fog, and Cinda has learned to greet it in the morning with a nod. She tiptoes into the kitchen to feed the cat. She's lost the illusion that it understands her and no longer tries to communicate with it through speech. She strokes its back from time to time.

Cinda doesn't know how he did it, but he taught her silence. Her—weaver of words and worlds, singer of songs, teller of tales, asker of questions. As they sprung from her lips, he collected her words in a burlap sack and buried them in the backyard in the middle of the night. No marker, no cross, no flowers on alternate Sundays. He sprinkled grass seeds over the grave, and she has been unable to locate her words since. She searches her house for a treasure map, but has not found one yet. She doesn't know where to reach John. She doesn't know what she'd say or what sort of ransom to offer. He's holding her words hostage. He left her with her body. Bastard.

My oh my, the old lady with the whistling nose chirps as the construction worker stretches his legs out across the aisle and then slides off the seat to the floor. She pokes his shoulder with the tip of her umbrella, and he wakes up with a start. He looks no one in the eye as he lifts himself back into his seat. He notices his fly is open and blushes, pulling his jacket down over his hardness. Cinda stares right at him and chokes back a laugh. Her laugh would kill him, that's how powerless he feels right now. Caught sleeping, vulnerable, aroused. Perhaps he's a sleep-talker and is afraid he has let slip his deepest, darkest secret and his lover's name, and that his fellow riders will impart this information as small-talk as soon as they get off the bus. Cinda pushes her lips out the window and opens her mouth. The laugh escapes without a sound and soils someone's windshield like a large mosquito. The wipers smear it and then wipe it away.

She did not speak as John packed his belongings into green garbage bags. No tears fell from her eyes. Dust rose from the throw rug as he rolled it up and hoisted it under his arm. Cinda sneezed into her hand, and he said bless you. She opened her mouth to reject his blessing and sneezed again. Bless you, bless you, bless you. Nothing more to say to each other. She didn't want his blessing. It felt more like a curse. She laughed in his face when he tried to embrace her, and then slammed the door shut. These were the only sounds she could still make.

She walked around the apartment after she heard the outside door click shut, stepping around the empty spaces that were once occupied by his objects. The only thing he left behind was a pair of rubber gloves—a cheap orange reminder of hands that would never touch her again. That was how John communicated, in slow gestures and precise caresses, perfected to the point of language.

He would ambush her from behind in the middle of the day and fill her mouth with a handful of grapes. He would then push up against her, pulling up her shirt and his so their nipples could fuck, so the heat of his flesh could sear hers, so their bodies could pucker, fart, and slide—friction, moist skin on skin. This move always stunned her silent.

"I have shaved the whiskers on my chin and cheeks so I can plant my smooth face between your thighs," he once declared in a rare phone conversation on a day her body didn't feel like talking. It was no idle promise. There had been more intense conversations between her cunt's flapping lips and John's tongue than they had ever had in their year together. Some people would not think this was a problem.

But Cinda's body was mute when they met. It had been betrayed, its needs stifled too many times, so it retreated, clamped shut like an oyster, refusing to share its pearls with anyone. Its orgasms, if they dared come out at all, whispered. She had to repeat the words for John to make sure that he didn't completely miss them. Her body's signs had to be read as carefully as lips, tracked as attentively as she wrote down his sparing words in her journal. Just as her body started making its first sounds, he left.

She picked up the orange gloves with her fingernails and tossed them into the trash can to fester with brown banana peels and fish carcasses. She then crawled into her bed, under the covers, and disappeared into the gap. She didn't emerge until today. She had no choice. The smell of decay was making her ill.

Her stop, and she pushes her way towards the door. It is pouring now, and water gushes past the sidewalk and into the sewer. Cinda attempts a short leap from the bus to the sidewalk, but lands in a puddle anyway. She is soaked to the knees. Damp and rotting. Other passengers push past her as she shakes the water out of her shoes. The businessman with the turquoise trenchcoat shoves her out of his way and drops a leather glove at her feet. She picks up the glove and goes after him, holding her umbrella out in front of her like a shield against the wind and rain. Against decomposition.

The businessman turns onto a side street that Cinda has never taken before—a street where bodies are exchanged for dollars, no questions asked—and disappears. Cinda puts on his glove and strokes the back of her neck. She walks past a young whore who is wearing white shorts that are shrinking up her ass, exposing the chafed half-moons of her cheeks. The whore looks anxious and cold, unsure of why she's standing in the rain. She too is decomposing, rivulets of green make-up streaking down her face, her bleached hair limp and wet, her thigh-high black boots scuffed and leaking. Cinda watches from behind a lamppost as the whore approaches one stopped car, then the next, but does not get in; her posture slumps more with every rejection. It starts to rain harder and Cinda's whole body is screaming half-formed words and instructions that she can hardly decipher. She shuts her umbrella and moves towards the melting woman. She is afraid of what has come over her, but she keeps walking anyway. She couldn't stop now even if she wanted to.

She offers the whore her umbrella, but she refuses it. Cinda holds out a twenty-dollar bill with her gloved hand. The whore looks around, then pulls Cinda into an alleyway and asks her what she wants. Cinda slides the crisp bill down her halter-top, cups a breast in the wet leather of her palm, and squeezes. She opens up her own coat and lifts her shirt, pushing her breasts up against the whore's. She explores the whore's body as if it were her own, dragging nails up a thigh, scraping an earlobe with her teeth. Cinda teaches her, through example, what will make her body cry out—all the things that John taught her. The whore catches on quickly and follows Cinda's movements. For a moment the two women stare into each other's eyes, then turn away, embarrassed.

As they slither and press against each other, Cinda thinks of the mirror and the fifteen-year-old girl staring at herself, touching the parts of her body that hum. Her hand finds its way into the whore's shorts and her fingers slide against the smooth wetness of her cunt, grinding the clitoris between the joints of her fingers. The whore reaches up Cinda's dress, mirroring her moves. Neither of them makes a sound. Cinda's body convulses in silent orgasm, followed instantly by the whore's moans. Cinda draws the whore's tongue into her mouth and bites down on it until it bleeds. The whore gasps, more out of shock than pain, swears and pushes Cinda away. She then adjusts her costume, slips the twenty into her boot, and goes back to the curb as if nothing has happened. Cinda watches her dab her bloodied tongue with a wrinkled hand-kerchief, spit red on the sidewalk. She stares sadly at the whore sadly as she tries, unsuccessfully, to make eye contact with the drivers of slow-moving, passing cars.

As Cinda stumbles out of the alleyway, she spots the businessman in the turquoise trenchcoat hunched over his dick in a doorway, beating it towards her. He laughs in her face as she watches him, paralyzed. He yammers like a monkey as a stream of come sprays the pavement by her feet. Cinda strips off his glove and whips it at him, then runs back onto the busy street, where people are engaged in cordial conversation. Where lives have gone on, unaware of her corruption, indifferent to her grief.

She turns around abruptly, as if a disembodied hand has tapped her on the shoulder. She sees John across the street, ranting like a lunatic, yelling at strangers, chattering manically to the man at the newsstand. He is spilling words as if he had them to spare. Her words. Her windpipe constricts. She opens her mouth to yell his name, to tell him to stop, to give her words back, but his name sticks in her throat like a fishbone, and the rest of the words come up as bile. She draws her tongue back into her mouth, swallows hard, and presses her lips shut. The bone remains lodged in her throat and her eyes fill with rain. She changes her route, forgetting her destination. She sleepwalks the city streets for the rest of the day, crashing into strangers, wading through puddles, sitting on curbs, and crying into gutters.

That night, she tears up the back yard with her fingers and teeth. She excavates under the house and into the front yard. She digs like a rabid squirrel in mid-winter until the skin on her fingers is pulled back to the bone. She sifts through the grass and dirt with a silver spoon. She finds remnants of the burlap sack and a few of her words scattered, one under a rock, three beneath the porch. She places them in her mouth and sucks on them until they course through her veins. She repeats the words incessantly, like a little girl's skipping-rope mantra, until they lose all sense, all meaning. She then goes inside, sits down on the floor, wraps her arms around herself, and howls—for the words she may never recover, for the meanings that are no longer hers.

Peanut Butter, Figs, and Swollen Lips

THERE IS THIS YOUNG MAN I see on the bus on mornings when our individual lateness coincides. He looks about sixteen, give or take a few months. He is a tall, angular man-foetus with a haircut like a blond sumo wrestler. On some days he carries a guitar case, the ultimate prop. He leans on it when he stands, rests it between his thighs when he gets a seat, and talks around it when he's with friends. I sometimes wonder if he actually plays guitar or just carries around the empty case to impress girls. When I was his age, I had a friend who did just this. If anyone asked to see it, he would calmly explain that this particular guitar was a heat-sensitive instrument and could not be exposed to the dank night air as it would self-destruct. I will assume that this young man plays his guitar passionately, composing love ballads full of four-letter words for blossoming fourteen-year-old girls.

I have given him a name because lately I have begun to consider him mine. He belongs to me in that intangible way that people who see one another constantly but never speak become acquainted with the other's wardrobe, posture, and reading habits. I've never seen him read, but I know his pointy leather shoes on feet that look too big for his skinny frame. They are a faded red, with too many scuffs and not enough polish. Polish in that shade must be hard to find, and I couldn't imagine him polishing his shoes. I could walk onto that bus and never look above anyone's knees and recognize him.

Young man, I name you David, for creation, and beauty, and youth. You are not beautiful, David, but when I put down my pencil, my paint, my chisel, you will be the most beautiful creature on earth, because you are mine.

Were I fourteen, David would love me, and I would love David. We would go to school holding hands and have late-night phone conversations from under the covers of our respective beds; long, intense discussions about nothing in particular. We would grope in dark alleys, in basements, at the movies, not daring to touch those private parts, but occasionally brushing up against them. We would get embarrassed, then excited, then perturbed, not really knowing what to do next, so we'd kiss between classes until our lips swelled.

My first love wrapped around me at fourteen. He was older by a whole year. He played basketball and wore tight, perfectly faded jeans. He took me to my first dance bar, a place set up for teenagers, dark and loud, where we could pretend we knew all that there was to know. He and I never had sex. It was never even a question. We would lie on my mother's black-and-green-striped couch, knocking into each other's teeth and bruising our lips. At school we held hands in the hallway even though it embarrassed us both. We'd neck at the movies and share plates of greasy fries afterwards at the dingy diner where all the kids hung out, smoking, flirting, wasting time. We'd talk on the phone for hours, speaking of everything and nothing, late into the night from the safety of our own beds. He was my boyfriend, I was his girlfriend, and no one else mattered.

Years later, I ran into my first love, by chance, in a pub with polished tables, brass lamps, and waitresses in too-short skirts. Over beer, pretzels, and talk of our past, my former high school sweetheart let drop, casually, that mine weren't the only lips to bruise in conjunction with his. What was a hot-blooded young man to do with his accumulated fervor after hours on my mother's couch, grinding up against me and exchanging enough saliva for a transfusion? He hoped he hadn't upset me, he said, noticing my clenched smile and the pretzels crumbling in my fist. I was so sweet and pure that he hadn't wanted to risk hurting me. So he fooled around with someone else instead, a girl I hated and whose knowing smirk during gym class now made sense.

A silence hung over our table like a swinging poker lamp, illuminating my face with its frozen smile, then his. He cleared his throat nervously, and the blood drained from his cheeks as I baptized him with my pint of beer. Cancel that dream.

In this life, David goes to high school, I go to work. I have imagined bringing David to work with me. He could sit by me in my cubicle, blushing whenever I introduced him to someone. He's a weird-looking kid and I'm a weird-looking adult, so no one would question his presence. People would think he was my cousin, or my nephew, or some friend of the family I was entertaining for the day. I imagine him reading the comic strips on my wall and not really understanding them, or flipping through a few papers on my desk disinterestedly. I see him rifling through my files, purposely left open, and finding this story. He begins to read it, then stuffs it back into the drawer willy-nilly when I come back with our root beers (we've got them in the pop machine in the cafeteria), unable to suppress his grin. He'd be bored at my office—*I'm* bored at my office—but we could smile at each other like two snakes in cahoots, waiting to death-wrap around each other.

I talk about him to everyone, this hero of my silent movie. I tell people how I pretend not to notice that he sits closer to me on the bus as time goes by. He waits until I've settled and then chooses his position. I smile into my dummy book and he looks straight ahead. What I really want to do is grab him by the collar of his tattered leather jacket and plant a hot and juicy kiss on his mouth in front of all his friends, all his teachers. But I don't tell anyone about that part. He pretends not to care as he's leaving the bus, then turns around and stares at me before the doors shut behind him. I've even seen him walk through the big empty schoolyard looking back brazenly at me. How much is that girl/woman in the window, bark, bark. I return the stare and smile. At squinting distance, it's safe to be lovers.

The girls who hover around David on the bus have a tone I remember: a combination of teenage immortality and new-found sexuality that bursts the seams of their too-tight jeans. They touch him lightly when they speak, leaning in closely so he can catch a whiff of their perfume, then throw back their heads in laughter so their hair dances in the morning sun. Womanhood: courtesy of Silkience, Flex, and Pert. It is uncontainable, their teenage passion. It is unleashed proudly, joyfully—an excited puppy dragging its master through the park, stopping to sniff every tree. It is also the biggest crock in the book. Promises with no idea of how to fulfill them. A naked hook, a play-dough tart, a little girl in mommy's gestures. The younger boys don't realize what's hit them. They know they feel something strange and tingly in their sloppy pants that makes their faces burst magenta for no apparent reason, but they put it down to the tuna fish sandwiches they ate for lunch. The older boys demand payment.

I've never slept with a sixteen-year-old. When I was fourteen, there was mild petting up against cold, brick walls in schoolyards on wet nights, but no penetration except for clumsy attempts by anxious fingers. If a hand wormed its way down my skin-tight jeans, pulling various pubic hairs out of their sockets, then tried to ram its grubby digits up an opening that did not seem to exist, I would grab it and, in a panic, whisper, "That hurts, I'm a virgin," then look away. I was not proud of my virginity; it was just my weapon against total destruction. Some boys would withdraw, while others would try to hang their manhood around my neck, or tuck my virginity into their wallet to pull out and display like a lewd photo passed around the boys' locker room.

By sixteen, sixteen-year-old boys were too young for me. I had to aim higher and be penetrated. I finally gave my virginity to a collector, which was a mistake. I should have given it to someone who had never seen one before and would lock it away safely in a velvet-lined jewel box. Every once in a while, he could carefully lift it out of its protective case, smell it, feel it, reminisce about what it looked like when he first saw it, then put it away. It would always be safe and dry. It would not tarnish or fade away. It would not lie in a heap with a hundred other collectibles.

My first screw was massage and whiskey induced. It had nothing to do with love, flowers, or fireworks. Necessity over desire. My virginity weighed me down. It was awkward, unwieldy, and embarrassing. The impacted wisdom tooth of my youth. Sex was a thing to get over with, there wasn't supposed to be anything fun about it. There was, of course, the forbidden fruit aspect, but that could have been satisfied by any number of vices, all offering imminent death by disease, overdose, or by murder when my mother found out. The power of refusal never even occurred to me.

I stood alone in my mother's kitchen, swallowing warm, amber poison to make myself numb. Angelface was already naked and in my bed when I got there, flipping through my diary and smiling because he'd found himself in it. Calm and cocky, he held out the covers and invited me in.

The event itself was disappointing. After he heaved and ho'd and writhed and panted and made a mess all over my Mickey Mouse sheets, he squinted at me through the near-darkness and asked the eternal question: "Did you like it?" This question bounced around in my sixteen-year-old brain, accumulating information about other things I'd liked in the past, like peanut butter and massages, figs and kissing. As I compared the event to those established pleasures, the only answer I could muster was a question itself. "You mean that was it?" Beeeep. Wrong answer. Go to the back of the class. Sit in the corner. Give back your gold star. I couldn't see Angel's face through the darkness, but I knew the second the words tumbled from my lips that it was all over.

This is why David and I should keep our love pure. The moment penetration is achieved, something is lost. Someone is disappointed, someone's interest wanes, and then the lies begin. The "I'll call you tomorrow" lie. The "I love you" myth. I was too young for sex. David is too young. You must get older before you know how to be young properly. That's what I can offer David, hindsight on a platter.

But that's not what he wants from me. David wants to be a man. A man in a movie filled with blue smoke and dim lights. A man waking in his lover's bed, tangled in wrinkled white sheets and tired limbs. He brushes her hair away from her sleeping face and stares at her, drinking in the softness of her features, the innocent pucker of her mouth. She becomes a five-year-old when she sleeps, trusting and sweet. She hugs him in her dreams and smiles. He tickles her ear with a strand of her hair, and she shifts her head and scratches, grumbling softly. He kisses her ear and she wraps her arms around his neck, her legs around his waist. She is not awake. She engages in somnambulistic sex where she can proceed without inhibition, without expectation. Nothing can remove her from the present moment because there is nothing else. She smiles and growls, she nibbles on his cheeks. Her hands explore his landscape without hesitation; she climbs his peaks, slides down valleys. She looms over his body, a thundercloud on all fours, but her eyes are closed, her mind is closed, and when he lifts his body towards her, when he begins to penetrate her state, she wakes up abruptly, and it's over. The spell is broken, the magic is soaked up by the sheets. And David becomes sixteen again. He doesn't know what he did wrong. He doesn't know what to do next. And then the lies begin.

I would like to undress David and let him stand naked in the afternoon light of my bedroom window. I would like David to undress me, slowly, with trembling hand and red face, careful not to touch any private parts. I'd like his teenage skin to brush against mine. He is hesitant, afraid to make the wrong move, wondering how far he should go, where the line is drawn. We touch and kiss until our lips swell, and then slowly pull on our clothes, not daring to desecrate the temple of our pure love by sweat, grunts, or disappointment.

None of this will ever happen because I've been forewarned by someone who used to be a young man that even speech between David and I would desecrate the temple of our love. I would remember what sixteen-year-old boys were really like, and he would find out that I am twenty-six and have figured him out. A tension would form between us, throwing us at opposite ends of the now too-small bus. The anticipation of our morning meetings would turn into unspeakable dread, sending him to school earlier, me to work later. Or we would both try to avoid each other by being either early or late and would relentlessly keep bumping into each other. Eyes would fix on the floor of the bus, and we would ricochet off the tension in separate directions. That would be tragic, so I don't speak to him, though I think about it constantly.

Imaginary Conversation #1:
David sits directly across from me on the bus. We both look up at the same time and our eyes meet. Since we can no longer avoid each other, I smile an inviting smile. David smiles back.

David (blushing slightly): Hi.

Me: Hi there, I was wondering how long it would take you to actually speak to me.

Beeeep. Wrong answer. Young David blushes an extreme tomato shade and scuttles to the door of the bus, getting off five stops ahead of school and pretending to enter a stranger's house. I stare at him out the window until he becomes a leather-clad pin-prick in the bus route horizon. He never takes that bus again, but skulks around the subway platform until he is certain I have been whisked away, preferring to wait for the next bus and the perpetual detention his lateness ensures to the humiliation of being totally predictable to an older woman. He does not realize that not appearing ever again is as banal as saying hello two months down the line. It's nearly the end of the school year anyway, so he takes comfort in the fact that he won't have to face me until fall. And maybe, if he's lucky, I'll have quit my job by then. Or his parents will suddenly decide to move the family unit to another city where my presence as testimony to his stunted prowess will become a faded memory that is bleached out immediately whenever it colours in. He will continue to have problems speaking to strange women throughout his adult life, leading to many nights out with the boys, a few disastrous blind dates where he says nothing out of fear of being predictable, and the development of an acute nervous tic that makes his nose twitch whenever he finds himself inadvertently staring at any woman he doesn't know.

Imaginary Conversation #2:
I rush onto the bus just as it is about to lurch off the platform. I spot one empty seat in the last row and make a bee-line for it. My morning legs give way and I topple into the lap of plastic and vinyl comfort. As I regain my bearings and the a.m. mist clears from my eyes, I notice that fate has planted me next to David. The sleeve of his leather jacket brushes against the sleeve of mine, and I cannot help but smile. David smiles back.

David (blushing slightly): Hi.

Me: Hello.

David: Nice day.

Me: Not bad.

David (suddenly dropping to one knee and pulling a bouquet of wilted flowers from his guitar case): Where do you go, my love, after I leave you stranded on this lonely, desireless bus? I think of you all day long while I sit in Math, English, Sex Ed., imagining you on a chaise lounge conducting important business on a speaker phone. Please take me with you. I ask for nothing but to worship you from afar. *(He hugs my calf and rests his head on my knee, closing his eyes and trembling in adoration.)*

Me: My young prince, if only the years were not so cruel as to divide us so. If only I could draw you into a rose-petalled world where we could sleep the sleep of the pure, and touch lips with our eyes and imagination. *(The back of my hand rests up on my forehead. I speak towards the bus ceiling.)* Oh, cruel fate that has given you five years too few and me, five years too many. I shall go into cryonic suspension until your mind and body catches up to mine in years. I only ask, my lily prince, that you guard me from grave robbers, blackouts, and indifference, and that you remain as pure for me as you are now. When I defrost, we shall be equal and, I hope, able to live out our love in a warmer clime.

I fall to my knees and we embrace right there on the bus. We smile cheek-to-cheek smiles into the camera, and I am frozen in time while he ages rapidly. The rest of the passengers fade into blackness as the dusty pink light of our new-found love intensifies. The camera pulls away out the window, and the bus drives off into a heart-shaped sunset.

Probable Conversation:
I am standing in the bus. I am late for work and recognize the rest of the chronically late crowd. The bus starts to roll away from the platform, and I see David running beside it, banging on the doors with his fist. The bus driver hits the brakes, and the standing passengers, including me, topple over. David pushes his way through the grumbling crowd and stops right next to me. We stand back to back for a few seconds and then turn towards each other at the same time. I smile at him and think, It's now or never.

Me: Hi.

David (smiles and blushes): Hi.

Me: Do you get in trouble when you're late?

David: Nah, they're kind of used to it by now.

Me: Yeah, it's good to train them early. What are you studying?

David: Music. Composition.

Me: Wish I'd done something like that in high school. What do you play?

David: Classical guitar in school, hardcore with my band.

Me: Good combination. Sort of yin/yang.

David: Are you into music?

Me: Some of my friends are, so I know a few things.

David: Here's my stop. Nice talking to you. See ya around.

Me: Yeah, see ya.

He gets off the bus and walks backwards across the street, smiles, and waves. I smile and wave back. The school bell rings, and he turns around and runs through the empty schoolyard. He looks so fragile in the open space that I fear for his safety when I think of all the people who are going to hurt him as he grows up. I'm glad I've spoken to him. I'm glad he's interesting. I'm sad I'm not fourteen.

But I know that even if I were fourteen, David might not love me. There was no perfection, no purity, no Prince Charming looking for his Sleeping Beauty at fourteen. No one was allowed to remain Snow White for long. The boy whose name littered my copybooks and every desk I sat at never asked me to the prom. Or if he did, I paid for it somehow, sometime, with body or spirit, even years later. Everyone deserves a moment when all her dreams come true. When her heart can leap right out of her body and glide with the butterflies, flitter with the ladybugs, sing with the crickets. Just one second of absolute joy in the grand scheme of things before routine lumbers in with its fly swatter.

One day, when I'm very late for work, by the type of coincidence that brings fated lovers together, David walks out onto the sunny platform. No one is there but the two of us. We watch each other carefully through stolen glances. I close my constant book and wait. For the bus, for him to do something, for anything. Our eyes meet and I smile. He smiles back and blushes. With my hand, I call him closer, as if I have a secret to impart that must be guarded even from the walls of the subway platform. As he approaches, I notice the sun bouncing off his peach-fuzz chin. I smell Ivory soap and shoe polish. I glance down at the familiar footwear, then I study his face. The age cracks in his leather jacket do not erase his adolescent blemishes.

His eyes zig-zag. He looks nervous, but happy. Excited and tingly. If I touch him, I might get a shock. If I kiss him, I'll be electrocuted. I debate in those last seconds whether to grab him by the collar and kiss him full on the mouth or to give him a shy peck on the cheek. I stare at the curves and crevices of his ear. He stands there waiting. I stand there paralyzed. He does not realize that at this very instant both our wishes have come true and passed each other in the night. I have become fourteen again. I am not in control and I look for a cue. I am unsure of the relevance and the appropriateness of my action. I have not considered the consequences. I am unprepared. I have forgotten the condoms, clean underwear, breath mints, an alibi. I do not have the time before curfew, the nerve to say yes, the desire to say no. My face breaks out and I slouch. My arms are suddenly too long for my body. I blush and stare at my feet. I shrink into puberty and my clothes don't fit. David notices. He immediately grows to six-foot-two and puts on twenty pounds. His peach fuzz becomes stubble, and his posture relaxes. He puts his arm around my shoulder and pulls me towards him. I feel pressured, excited, vulnerable, and it shows on my face. What will he do now that he's got me in his grasp? Would a nice girl even get herself in this predicament? My heart rat-tat-tats. He leans in and lightly touches my lips with his. He brings my hand to his mouth and gently kisses my knuckles one at a time. There is a knot in my stomach, and my knees are about to give way. I am swooning. People really do that type of thing.

What happens next has to do with buses, schedules, other public transit patrons, and work. These things are unimportant. What remains is a memory snapshot, an encapsulated moment in time and space when David became a man, or when the high school sweetheart I longed for crossed the street at the appropriate traffic light, or negotiated the right corner just in time to help me pick up my scattered schoolbooks. I have waited a long time for this moment. I will treasure it forever. Lock it away in an ornate box lined with blue velvet. I will wear the key around my neck, and every once in a while, I will take the moment out and polish it so it remains untarnished by time. It is unique. I didn't have one, and there will never be another quite like it.

A TASTE FOR MEAT

IT HAD STARTED SIMPLY, months earlier, right around the time Clarissa had begun settling into her new apartment with Zach—that is, after they'd resolved the petty arguments about sleep time and wake time, wall hangings and abominations of taste, and the proper means of disciplining the cat. Just when her life seemed to be recovering its normal flow, Clarissa noticed Zach's taste for raw steak emerging —filet mignon rare, wallowing in a pool of its own blood. She couldn't watch as he attacked the piece of cold meat, knife and fork ripping soft, pink flesh. She took her plate of steamed vegetables into the next room, sat on the floor, and ate with the cat. They always hide something, she confided to Baudelaire, who responded with his usual feline disdain. Zach offered no explanation.

In the weeks that followed, the bones of small animals began clogging up their trash compactor, which spewed bits of matted fur and splintered bone. Clarissa did not ask Zach where the bones came from or how they got into the sink. She scooped up the remains with a wooden spoon and pushed them deep into the drain while her stomach churned.

A few nights later she found the knife under Zach's pillow. She was stretching her arms out in half-sleep when the blade nicked her knuckle, waking her with its slippery, slow pain. As if he smelled her spilled blood, Zach woke up immediately and suctioned his lips to her wound, suckling away happily until her hand was a bluish white. He then fell into a thick, hazy sleep. Clarissa grabbed her pillow and a blanket and moved herself to the couch, pushing Baudelaire onto the floor. This was the first time that she and Zach had slept apart.

When confronted in the morning, knife pointed at his nose, Zach denied any intention to "carve her up and stuff her down the sink." He claimed he kept the knife under his pillow to protect him from nightmares, like a juju or a charm. He pulled out a chicken's foot from his bathrobe pocket and slid it behind his ear. "And this is for luck," he said, grinning broadly, "'cause I'm such a lucky guy." He leaned in for a kiss. Clarissa pulled back to avoid getting grazed, tapped the gnarled claw with her fingernail, then pushed it away from her face. As she kissed him back, her toes curled.

The next night, she turned over to stroke Zach's hair, but he was gone. She found him out in the living room, sitting by a candle and poking his fingertips with a needle. She cringed as he raised his hand above his head, letting slow droplets of blood fall into his open mouth. Clarissa went back into the bedroom and locked the door. Zach scraped at it and cried, trying to dig through to the other side, while Baudelaire observed unsympathetically.

"We need a counselor," Clarissa told Zach the next morning. "This is not normal."

"We don't need a counselor," Zach replied. "You need to bite me, to feast on me. If you bite me, all will be well. If you loved me you would." He then confessed that he longed for the sight of his blood running down her chin, her teeth stained red like a lioness after the kill. He said he wanted to feel desired. Was this not, after all, what love was about?

They always hide something.

Now, Clarissa didn't even eat meat. Fatty flesh ground between her teeth, communing with her tongue like some long lost relative was a horror she had done without for many years. She'd hesitated when Zach asked her to move in with him because she knew it would mean the odour of cooked flesh impregnating the walls, the curtains, the bed. They had made a deal that meat, when cooked, would only be cooked outside on the barbecue. They also agreed that she would not try to convert him to her vegan lifestyle, and that he would not try to push his meat on her. Until now, their pact had remained unchallenged, their truce had held. But suddenly Zach was asking Clarissa to become a meat-eater. He wanted her to eat him.

Clarissa pondered the situation carefully because she loved Zach more than she had ever loved anyone else. She didn't even feel the need to compile a list of why Zach should be loved by her. Her love for him was so complete and pure that she had stopped trying to compartmentalize the beauty of it long ago. She loved his mass, his depth, and his circumference. Anything else was just details which had more to do with quizzes in women's magazines than with the scope of her love for Zach. If she were to eat any man it would certainly be Zach, since she was sure his flesh was sweet and lean, his blood refreshing as a glass of watermelon juice on a hot day, as rich and pungent as a cup of spiced burgundy on a frigid winter's night. Sometimes, when she looked at Zach, she wanted to swallow him whole, like some backwards Zeus, so she could feel his whole being inside her, so she could think his thoughts. She wanted to carry him like an unborn child she could feed and who fed off her. Zach was so well-suited to her that she often felt she had created him in her own image, filled him with her desire. She did not like disappointing him.

But to draw his blood was not something Clarissa had ever wished to do. The sight of her own blood dripping out of her into the toilet every month filled her with dread. She could not help but think that her life was running out of her drop by drop, month by month. Like some punishment from the gods that was no longer questioned, she was allowed to gradually bleed to death.

Zach, on the other hand, had become very enthusiastic about the arrival of her blood as of late. Clarissa normally refused physical contact during her cursed week, but had been caught bleeding without her knowing it. When Zach reached between her legs and brought back a red finger for the first time, a light seemed to shine out of his eyes. He kept reaching back inside for more sacred paint, as he called it, and he drew mystical symbols all over his own body and hers—curly crosses and tear-filled eyes. She would have stopped him, she was so ashamed of her bloodshed, but he seemed so incredibly happy, as if all at once he had discovered his long lost art.

He began to keep track of her cycle as if it were his own, and the menstrual painting became an elaborate ritual accompanied by trance states and guttural chanting. Clarissa squirmed, but forced a smile as Zach finger-painted their bodies, then their faces, the floors, the windows, and finally the bedroom walls with her blood—one symbol every month staining the walls like a growth chart of their love. It was not long after this that he asked to taste it. Clarissa forbade it, but Zach's craving was unanswerable. First he smeared a red fingertip across his lips, the tip of his tongue carefully picking up the sticky residue. He pronounced it fresh and salty, like mineral water. Soon he was holding champagne flutes, then beer mugs under her gush. He toasted the moon and drank her slough in one shot, not wasting a drop. Clarissa refused to kiss him afterwards. Her duty was to release the blood and die, she told him. Taking it back would go against nature.

Zach had no sympathy for nature. Nature was an unjust mother, granting women the power to bleed without death, while condemning men to mortal servitude. He had yearned for a passageway into the secrets of blood loss ever since his little sister, at the age of eleven, had called him into the bathroom to witness her passing. "It won't be long now," she sniffled, pointing at the pinkish water in the bowl. Zach, who was six, started to cry. When their mother came home and found her children sobbing over the toilet bowl, she laughed and hugged his sister. She explained to both of them that this blood was a blessing, and that his sister was now a woman. They celebrated that night, piercing his sister's ears with a needle and placing rose-scented sachets in her underwear drawer. From then on things changed between Zach and his sister. She became secretive and dismissive, and he was no longer allowed to sleep in her bed. Longing for the secret that engendered the change, Zach cut himself with his mother's shaver in several sensitive places to initiate his own passing. His blood, however, was not met with celebration.

But at last, through Clarissa's flesh and blood and her perfect love, Zach believed he could be released. Their sex life changed rapidly. No longer was Zach interested in penetration, nor did he care for the softness between Clarissa's legs when it was not an open wound. Even then, he no longer caressed her thighs or tickled her toes. He stopped quaffing her vital fluids like a victorious viking and, instead, performed a series of gynecological tests on her, pressing his thumb to her belly like a ketchup dispenser and collecting her blood in beakers. He'd study its colours and textures with cotton swabs, taking careful notes in a big black book before sucking each and every beaker dry. Only on the nights she bled did

Clarissa know his whereabouts. The rest of the month he was absent for large chunks of the night, covered in dirt and bruises upon his return, and mysterious when questioned. He spent hours in the bathroom after he got home, cleaning himself and humming, but Clarissa decided not to open that door.

If it had been anyone but her perfect Zach, and if Clarissa was less sure of his love for her—which he had once described as the attainment of his life's goal—she might have suspected that he had found other women to satisfy his blood lust. The recurrence of the animal carcasses in the sink comforted her in a strange way. But her tolerance was running short, and the knife was still under the pillow; let's not forget the knife. She demanded that the knife be returned to its proper place in the kitchen. Zach refused. He was tired of her rejection, he spat back. He sat on Clarissa's belly and placed the sharp end of the blade on his wrist.

"If I cut myself," he threatened, "will you let me bleed to death? After all these months that I have honoured your lost blood, drinking it so it wouldn't be wasted, decorating the walls to commemorate its passing, will you let mine be lost forever? Will you let me die?"

Clarissa answered that her blood loss was not intentional, but was a punishment from the gods, a slow death, not self-inflicted. When twelve-year-old Clarissa showed her mother her blood-stained panties for the first and last time, her mother draped the house in black velvet and wept inconsolably for the passing of her youth. Clarissa began to cry, too, as she stuffed tissues between her legs, assuming that the grieving was for her. She had not been prepared for the wonders of womanhood; the secret had never been passed on. Though she came to realize that she would survive the monthly hemorrhage as if nothing had happened, she played out her death throes every time she bled, surrounding the bed with red votive candles, laying herself out in a white gauzy nightdress, and making peace with her various gods.

Clarissa reminded Zach of her cyclical trauma and begged him to go back to sleep. He could keep the knife if it meant so much to him. He could get ten or twenty knives and dangle them over the bed with string, like wind chimes, to scare away the dead. She loved him dearly, but couldn't take much more. This was the sanest relationship she'd ever been in, and she didn't want to see it end this way. She promised to try some sausage in the morning.

Belly-perched Zach did not move, except to push the knife's tip into a vein. He shut his eyes and stiffened his jaw as the tip dug deeper into his wrist. At first there was no blood, as if the shock of the cut was not yet believed by his flesh. Then a fat, dark red drop oozed out, splashing like oil onto Clarissa's left breast. She stared at Zach, his eyes still squeezed tight, as his life drained all over her torso. He looked so pale compared to the blackness of his blood that she was afraid he might die, right there on top of her, because his blood had nowhere to go. She began to cry for the loss of him, for her inability to drink his blood, to save him. Zach swayed back and forth, moaning and calling out Clarissa's name, holding his cut wrist closer and closer to her mouth. A drop slid in past her lips as she wept, and Clarissa was instantly reminded of her perfect and complete love for Zach. If it were to remain perfect and complete, she understood, it would have to include his flesh, his blood, the smell of his shit, the taste of his piss.

She suctioned her mouth to his wrist and drank and drank until drinking Zach's blood was no different than swallowing her own saliva. Until she was so full of his blood, she felt she had been replenished of her own and all her dying had been erased. And if she kept drinking it, she all at once knew, she would become younger and younger. She would go back to an age before blood is lost, and she would finally become immortal.

Zach, of course, his wish fulfilled, came violently, spraying the symboled walls, turning the dried brown blood red again. Clarissa bound his wound with a sanitary napkin and Zach fell asleep happy, cradled in Clarissa's arms.

Baudelaire padded out quietly and never returned.

Zach is still the only man Clarissa will eat because she loves him. And with their reciprocal blood transfusions, they will be sustaining each other for a long time to come. That is, after all, what love is about. Clarissa can't bring herself to eat small animals yet—all that squirming and those little screams. But the back of Zach's neck is raw with her teeth marks, and the more she bites him, the more blood he produces. She has acquired a taste for meat, you might say. Raw, juicy, freshly slaughtered.

Day Two Lasts
Twenty-Four Hours

DOMINA ATE HER YOUNG because she was depressed and they wouldn't stop screaming. They were scrumptious, those little rascals, and it cheered her up to find out that her flesh was so sweet.

The wind had been blowing out her curtains that morning, howling in her headache, and the clock on the wall had stopped. Domina buried her head under the covers and just wanted the day to go away, but little Billy wanted eggs and Mercutio wanted water. They were a bad reminder, those children, of their philandering father. Tramping around the world without a second thought for her.

She'd warned them, "Mummy will eat you for breakfast if you don't take care of yourselves right now." But they never listened. Instead, led on by Mercutio, they jumped onto the bed and bounced up and down trying to touch the ceiling. They hopped around the lump that was Domina under the covers and kicked her buttocks with their uncut toenails. And they laughed and laughed and snorted and laughed, ocean-sprays of spit raining down on the sheets.

"Get out of here, or I will devour you for my breakfast,"

Domina roared, the lump rumbling like an earthquake in an anthill. Baby boy breakfast was starting to sound like a tasty idea. Raw, or basted in the big turkey roaster? Potatoes and okra on the side?

The shadow of a large jungle bird swooped over the bed, and in the distance she could hear the chants of her people and their twig cutlery banging rhythmically against the sides of the cauldron. Today was a great feast day, celebrating the capture of two miniatures from enemy territory. And she, Princess Domina, most beautiful, desirable, and wild of all the women, would have her sacred innocence restored by taking the first bite. In a trance, she walked through the bugs and snakes to the clearing where her people exchanged news. She examined the apple-cheeked faces bobbing in the broth, crying and snotting, and smacked her lips. She placed her hands on top of their grease-matted bedheads and held them under until the bubbling stopped.

Then the phone rang and Mercutio answered. He mooed into the receiver and hung up.

She'd love to locate their lousy father and send him drumsticks or tiny pink penises in hot dog buns. He could share them with those sluts and trollops he'd left her for, then he'd dream a few strange things. After the first time they made love, he cawed in his sleep like a crow and later said he had been flying around her head trying to peck out her eyes while she snoozed. She had stared at him so intensely while he was coming that he'd lost his momentum and shriveled back to his side of the bed. She'd just wanted to make sure he wasn't faking. Shrivelling, she found out, was not a form of birth control.

Little Billy rode her rump and jammed his heels into her ovaries for stirrups. Mercutio sat on her shoulders, squeezing her neck with his bony knees. They exchanged kiddy conversation that meant nothing to anyone but them. Words like "popperator," "slimslime," and "roadrat." They also stuffed her last four tampons up their nostrils so they could play walrus.

Who were these insects, this body lice that she could not exterminate? These sign-language-beggar-cards that had been left at her table like unwanted kittens in sacks by the lake? Splash, the bag sinks to the bottom, and all you can hear is a few drowning mews and then nothing. None of her sisters would take on the task, but Domina didn't care. She didn't have a soft spot for small, cute things.

Domina met Igor at the cockfights. He was the man who cleaned up the blood and counted the feathers between rounds. He wore black rubber gloves and had a good ass. His job was very important on the cockfight circuit because in the case of a draw, where both cocks lay on their backs, claws in the air, plucked and bleeding but still breathing, the only way to determine the winner was through the scientific layout of the remains. Whichever side of the ring had more cock shrapnel determined the loser. Many fights broke out between the shrapnel judge and the cock owners, sometimes also involving spectators on the losing side of the bet. They would descend into the ring picking up stray feathers, trying to match them to their cock. Occasionally, they stepped on the head of the winning, half-dead cock in an attempt to quickly put it out of its misery and to overturn the judge's decision. But the judge's decision (the judge having trained as a high-turnover poultry sexer) was final. It was once suggested that natural death be the only tie-breaker, but cockfight fans are in it for the fast pace and did not like the idea of waiting around screaming at slowly expiring birds. Igor took pride in his work.

Domina waited for him one night after the last fight. She had lost every bet and her welfare cheque, and needed some comforting. She'd had her eye on Igor since the third fight when she saw him on his knees in the ring, smoothing out the dirt as if he were wrapping Christmas presents. Picking up dead birds and presenting them to their owners as if they were corsages. What else could a man like that do?

After the crowds left, Domina took off her clothes and lay in the ring, rolling around in the blood and feathers until they stuck all over her. One in her nostril made her sneeze. One between her thighs made her twitch. When Igor came around to clean, he thought that she was dead—one more of those crazy people who thought themselves cocks and pecked each other to death. He stood above her for a long time, wondering what to do. He had read about these situations in the training manual, but this was the first time he had been confronted by a bonafide "cockloon." He didn't remember the suggested etiquette. Handsome he was, but not quick. His solution was to clean her up and leave. This was exactly what Domina had devised—except for the leaving part.

He lifted the first feather carefully from her stomach, and his rubber fingertip stuck to her skin for an instant. He then moved up to her breasts and plucked away quickly, watching them jiggle under his deft movements like the heads of newborn puppies struggling in a box. He cautiously slipped his hands between her thighs, and he could have sworn that the dead woman smiled and moved her hips back and forth. He felt and overwhelming desire to plunge into the corpse, though he wondered if dead vaginas also had teeth, and whether it was written anywhere in the union manual that this was against the rules. He decided to clean her up, find the rule book, and then see if he still wanted to. He took out the sticky, witch's-wig mop, ran it over her body, starting at her toes and swirling it until it tickled her under the chin. In a low voice, he intoned ancient, grandmother mischief noises, "Babibooba, babibooba," and wondered if she would at least giggle. It always worked on him, though he was not dead, he reminded himself, just a bit slow.

The ticklefest left her dirtier, with mottled streaks of blood and cock droppings all over. Igor also thought she was starting to smell. In four snaps and a trip to the bathroom, he decided to fill a bucket with cold water (the better to preserve her with), and then drenched her. Aaaaaaah! She came back to life, jumping up and chasing him around the ring like a starving monkey chasing a banana kite. She scared the shit out of him, and now he could definitely smell something.

She was fast and mean. She jumped onto his back and bit into his neck. He let out a short cry and crashed down into the ring like a lead weight. She straddled him with her mighty thighs, holding him exactly where she wanted him. With one practiced hand, she tore off his pants. After it was over, she tied him up and carried him home over her shoulder.

Of course, this isn't exactly how Igor tells it over happy hour cocktails at the Casbah, but hey, this is Domina's story.

Ah, she remembered that day fondly, except for the fact that Billy and Mercutio now existed, twin diseases eating away at her life.

Igor escaped one dark and cold day, using the old, corner store, "I'll-be-back-in-a-flash-Dominakins-did-you-want-Rocky-Road-or-Neapolitan?" excuse during a very pregnant craving. His flash was more like seven cave carvings without the proper tools, and after a while, Domina understood what had happened. She didn't know what she hated him for more. She wrapped herself up in her blanket and went out into the streets, occasionally calling his name as if he were a lost dog, until she got to the ice cream counter.

Aaaaaaah! She was having one of those cravings right now. She erupted from under the covers, a naked virgin bellowing indecipherable curses and crawling out of the volcano. Her belly sagged with the memory of childbirth. She lifted it back into place, then let it drop again. Menstrual blood ran down her thighs, and a snow storm of goose feathers from a successful pillow fight covered her.

Billy and Mercutio fell to the floor, and she trapped them with the blanket. She carried them over her shoulder, plunged them in a tub of cold water, and held them under until they stopped screaming. She then scrubbed behind their ears and between their toes and banished them to their rooms for the rest of the day.

Day two was always the hardest.

She eventually took two aspirin, put on a sailor's dress and sandals, and had a café au lait. She didn't really eat her children; she was a vegetarian. Mostly, they took chunks out of her.

ANKLE-DEEP
IN MOONWATER

IT IS THREE A.M., AND THE indigo sky drapes the small white house by the sea with its darkness. The moon is shining full, and a ray of its smiling light falls into the window of the small white house and onto the face of the teenage guest. Though the air is warm and dry, the girl has pulled the covers up over the bridge of her nose. If a relative were to walk into the room to check on the girl, to make sure that the glass of water by her bed was filled, or to ascertain that she hadn't crawled out the window and into trouble, like so many girls her age were known to do, they would only see her tousled hair and her eyes squeezed shut as if against salt water.

Her body, hidden under the crocheted white cover, is balled up like a caterpillar whose belly has been poked with a stick. She gives the impression that she is in a deep sleep, her breathing giving way to a whimper or a moan reminiscent of a puppy dreaming. But she is not sleeping deeply. Half of her consciousness is guarding the object in her hand, which is buried under her pillow. In its tight fist, a small piece of plastic crackles, food wrap folded repeatedly until its transparency disappears and turns blue. Within the watery blue of the wrap are a few drops of red, shifting like mercury, breaking apart then rejoining. Throughout the night, as she struggles and fights in her half-sleep, she never lets go of the plastic. It is her only proof that something has happened.

A pain shoots through her pelvis, which involuntarily lifts slightly from the white sheets of the strange bed. She cries a little bit in her sleep and turns her body over, unconsciously hoping to rest it somewhere where it won't hurt anymore. The covers slide off as she turns over, and the moonlight kisses her swollen lower lip, bruised black and cracked with blood.

In a fairy tale or myth, by morning the bruised lip would be healed, the shooting pains would disappear, and everything would be restored to normal—rewound and erased by the power of that magical light coming down from the indigo sky. This does not happen.

She has finally escaped the interrogation from her relatives. She thought they would never let her go to the bathroom, and she needed to go so badly. Just to see what she looked like, to see what they saw when she walked through the door. She stares at herself in the mirror. It's worse than she thought, and she doesn't think they believed her excuses. She doesn't care. After tomorrow, her father will pick her up and she'll probably never see these people again. Last time she saw them she was a baby, and if she's lucky she'll be middle-aged by the time she's forced to look them in the eye again. She lets go of the waist of her pants and they fall to the floor. She pulls down her underwear and sits on the toilet. There are tiny drops of red on the white cotton crotch. She looks down into the water and more red is dripping out of her, bright red, not like menstrual blood, but a shiny red, like the blood of a gored bull. She reaches into her pocket and extracts the plastic wrapper from a sesame treat he bought her earlier that evening. Some of the honeyed seeds are still stuck to her teeth. She places the wrapper under her and catches a few drops of red. She studies the wrapper, sniffs it to see if there's any odour, but all she can smell is the residue of sesame seeds. She folds the wrapper carefully, making sure not to lose any of the drops, and places it on the edge of the sink.

That is when the first shooting pain rips through her insides. She bites her lip to keep herself from screaming out, but her teeth sink into the pulpy mess of the swelling that she momentarily forgot about. The scream gurgles in her throat, and a trickle of blood runs down her chin from her lip. Tears stream down her face, and she hobbles to the sink without lifting her pants to her waist—there is no point with the button and the zipper gone. As soon as she cupped her hands under the running tap to splash her face with cold water, which is what she does, her pants would fall to her ankles anyway. She dabs a piece of toilet paper to her lip and pats her face dry with one of their white towels. She is careful not to get any blood on the towel. They already hate her enough without her leaving traces on their linen. It's her fault, it is all her fault, she admits as she stares into the mirror. Stares until her face becomes unrecognizable to her. It is the face of someone she would not be friends with. A reject, a loser. Someone who deserved everything she got because she was a phony, a tease. Another shooting pain doubles her over, and she stumbles into her bedroom.

It is already past one a.m. and the relatives—the aunt and uncle she doesn't know—are waiting up for her in the small white house by the sea. They are tired and angry and not sure what they are going to do to her when she gets in. They are not certain what is within their rights as guardians of the girl for these few days, until her father comes to pick her up.

"Scandalous—what she's doing, how she's tarnishing our good name in the village," the aunt growls under her breath, not wanting to wake her daughters. The uncle nods slowly, silently in agreement. They introduced her to the mayor, and the priest, and the woman who owns the huge white hotel with the pool on the beach, the one reserved for the most affluent French tourists.

"What if someone sees her tonight, doing whatever she's doing with whoever she's doing it with? How will we hold our heads up with pride when we stroll through the town square next Sunday evening?" the aunt demands, her voice rising, her arm slashing the air, challenging the gods to answer her. Slut. Trollop. Whore. It was a bad hour when they said she could stay on with them for a few days after her father had to go back to work in the city. But it was family duty to open their home to her, and their daughters were so enamoured of "the cousin from America," they wanted to show her off to all their friends.

What were they thinking, letting her go off alone with their two children, little girls who could be poisoned by her example. The girls came back to their table in the square by themselves, sucking on lollipops they said some man bought for them—the same man their cousin left with. He was the brother of a friend of hers, their cousin had lied. Did she think they were stupid? They knew how these things worked.

"Maybe that's the kind of thing girls in America can get away with, but not in our village." The aunt stands in the doorway, hands on fleshy hips, squinting into the darkness, remembering. The uncle taps the end of an unlit cigarette on the coffee table, shakes his head and clicks his tongue, "tsk, tsk, tsk."

They don't know who to blame—her mother for bringing up such an ill-behaved animal, or her father who left his family before he could teach the girl right from wrong. No balls, that man. Runs around with foreigners half his age and can't even keep his daughter under control. What type of child did they expect him to have? She's perfect, the little bitch. Just what he deserves.

The relatives decide that they don't like her father either, and even though blood is blood, they will not be mingling with him in the future.

Just then the door creaks open and she walks in, disheveled, as if she's been rolling around in the corn fields and hasn't bothered to tuck her clothes back in properly, even as a gesture of respect. She begins babbling quickly, gaily, like she has done nothing wrong. Her hand is over her mouth, hiding a smirk. She is laughing at them, flaunting her defiance, and they will not have that under their roof.

"For however long you are here, you will adhere to the family rules," the uncle states authoritatively. "You will not wander the streets at night like a stray dog." The aunt grimaces at her, and harrumphs in accord.

She mumbles through her hand that she has been wandering the village lost for hours, trying to get home.

"How does that explain the grass stains on your pants?" her aunt spits out, her arms crossed, her foot tapping impatiently, counting time until an answer is offered. She resists the urge to yank the hand away from the girl's mouth.

She cut through a field thinking it was a shortcut, she answers quietly, and she fell. Her hand is still over her mouth and she is staring at her feet.

They don't want to hear anymore. They send her to her room,

informing her that her father will be picking her up tomorrow. They don't ask her if she has eaten. It never occurs to them to worry. They go to bed swearing that their daughters will never be given the chance to soil themselves like she did.

"I'll send them to a nunnery in the north to tend goats and to pray for their souls before I let a man touch them," the aunt vows. The uncle spits out the bedroom window of his little white house by the sea in disgust and looks up at the moon, which winks at him knowingly.

She stumbles out of the tall stalks of the cornfield and towards the road. Some of the stalks are taller than she is. Easy to get lost in, even when standing up. She is holding on to her pants where the button used to be. She's relieved that she wore her white sweater tonight, and that it's long enough to hide the broken zipper and the rip. She begins walking on the asphalt in the direction of the village lights. There are no cars on the road, so it must be very late, she figures. How is she going to explain the lateness of the hour to her relatives? She begins to walk faster, her sandals making a flip-flop echoing sound on the asphalt. She is not thinking about what just happened to her. She has no time to reflect at the moment. All she really wants to do is to get home to the strange bed in the little white house by the sea, crawl under the white sheets, and wait for tomorrow. He said he would meet her tomorrow at seven o'clock at the same place. He said he was so sorry he ripped her pants, but he would make it up to her. His sister owned a clothing shop in the city, and tomorrow he would give her the address so she could pick out a new pair of pants, a better pair than the ones she was wearing. A red pair, or maybe blue. She believes him. She cannot imagine at this point that he has no intention of being there. That he has walked off to meet his buddies for a beer to quench the thirst that their tussle has brought on. That he has long forgotten their date, her ripped pants, her name. She too wants something to drink. A glass of water, or some fresh orange juice to cleanse her palate of the dryness, of the pastiness and the sour taste left on her tongue.

She hears a car's motor in the distance and, for a moment, she feels saved. Maybe he's found his friend and they're coming to give her a lift back home. This is the instant when she realizes that her lip is throbbing. She touches it with her fingertips and it smarts. It feels like there is a pebble trapped under the skin. She runs her tongue over it, then folds her lip into her mouth, hoping to comfort it, to hide it. She starts formulating an excuse for the bruised lip, though she's not sure how noticeable it is, or whether or not it will be better by morning. She'll say that the guy's sister, her friend, was so surprised to see her that as she was waving her hands around in excitement, the huge green ring on her middle finger hit her in the mouth. Her friend felt very bad and made her hold ice against the lip so it wouldn't swell.

The car is right behind her now, and three men hang out the window cat-calling, making loud kissing noises and reaching out as if to grab her. Hey, baby. Hey, little girl. You want some? She jumps off the asphalt and onto the beach and starts to run, though her sandals are picking up sand, cutting her speed in half. She thinks she can still hear the men in the car calling to her, but it's only their echo in her ears combined with the crashing of waves. In her desperation to escape the calls, she trips over two bodies pressed into each other in the sand. A female voice calls her an idiot, while a male voice asks her if she wants to join in. The female starts yelling at the male, pushing him away, and calling him a wanker. The moon sheds an avenue of light onto the calm water, and she begins to run in that direction—away from the couple, away from the road. She plunges into the sea fully-clothed. The salt water stings her eyes, bites into her lip. As she emerges, the August wind picks up, and by the time she reaches the town square where ,she said goodbye to her cousins, she is completely dry.

She looks up from the square towards the identical white houses with their blinking lights on the hill, and realizes she has no idea which one belongs to her relatives. She has only been here two days and has never once been left alone to find her way. She chooses a road that she thinks she remembers and starts to climb. She spends the next two hours walking around the village, weaving down dirt roads and through fields of sheep. She peers through windows at sleeping girls and animals until she comes upon an empty bed that she assumes belongs to her. There is a light on in the front room, and she considers climbing through her bedroom window and directly into her bed, laid out with clean white sheets. But she has to go to the bathroom, so she must go through the living room anyway. She opens the front door quietly, hoping that they might not take notice, that they fell asleep hours ago, and that she will just be left in peace.

They are standing by the door, stony-faced, not even relieved to see her. She starts talking immediately, making excuses, hiding her lip. She doesn't expect forgiveness. She just doesn't know any other way to build a shield between these strangers and her pain.

Arm grabbed. Pull. Trip. Fall. Rocks pierce back. Corn stalks shudder. Button pops. Zipper breaks. Pants ripped to crotch. Bite lip. Forearm presses collarbone. Hands invade underwear. Yank to knees. Thumb jabbed in cunt. Middle finger in asshole. Fingers hooked. Pull. Rip. Tear. Unhinge. Insides fall out. Pain. Shooting. Burning. Tongue licks gums. Teeth crash. Bite lip harder. Unzip pants. Standing red cock. Outside pushes in. Cross legs. Wrench apart. Cross. Push away. Whimper. No. Can't. Virgin. No. Cock hits cheek. Mouth propped open. Push. Clench teeth. Push. Turn away. Knees squeeze neck. Thumb, middle finger pry teeth apart. Push. Slide. Push. Gag. Groan. Cry. Spurt. Swallow. Cry.

She is far enough from the square to let him hold her hand. She is thrilled that he has appeared. That he actually exists. Her whole face lights up when the skin of his palm touches hers.

They walk along the newly laid asphalt road in the last light of day. The moon is already out, impatient to take its place close to the earth. Close enough to touch or stroke its cheek. He helps her down off the asphalt and onto the beach. She leans on him to take off her sandals so that she can feel the warm sand between her toes. She can easily manage without his help, but she wants an excuse to press up against him. He grabs her chin and presses his lips against hers. His eyes are closed and his long lashes tickle her cheekbones. She closes her eyes and kisses him back harder than she's ever kissed anyone before. Her heart beats frenetically between her legs. He grabs her breast outside her shirt, and she pushes his hand away and moves back. Too fast, she thinks. Maybe she should be getting back to the village, she says, pulling him towards the road. Her excuse won't hold the relatives for long. They haven't been gone long, he assures her, and pulls her towards the water. She thinks about running away, but when she looks at his face, she is stunned by his beauty—the beauty of a Greek god, a statue chiselled in stone. How lucky she is to be blessed with his presence.

They stand ankle-deep in the cool water and he kisses her again, then lifts her by her armpits until her toes skim the surface. Her pant-cuffs drip salt. Let's make love, here on the beach, he purrs. Right here, right now. Isn't it romantic? She has to get back, she reminds him, and could he please put her down? His brow furrows and he pulls her towards the road. She trips over her feet a few times as he drags her across the sand. She brushes the sand off her soles and straps on her sandals. He has his back turned towards her, and she doesn't attempt to lean on him. She can sense he is angry, but he was rushing things a little. A kiss was just a kiss, and she had to get back.

He jumps onto the asphalt and lends her a hand. It is dark now, and the lights of the town seem very far away. She takes a deep breath that culminates in a deep sigh. He asks her what's wrong and she says she's late. He points to a car parked on the other side of the road, partially hidden by tall stalks of corn. He can drive her back if she'd like, he offers. It's his friend's car, and he has the keys. He brings out a key ring and jangles it like a dinner bell. He takes her hand and they cross the road. She doesn't have the time to look both ways. He squeezes her hand and she feels safe. How lucky she is that he noticed her today. Of all the girls on the beach, this godlike creature chose her. She squeezes his hand back and a tingly warmth rushes up inside her. Her round face glows like the moon.

As they approach the car, he drops his keys in the field. She bends over to help him look for them, but it is dark and she can't see a thing. He disappears among the stalks and she calls his name timidly, more like a question. His hand reaches out towards her, its fingers clamp around her wrist, and she is yanked into the stalks. It feels like her arm is momentarily disconnected from her shoulder before her body follows. The moonlight cannot penetrate the darkness amongst the stalks. She can no longer see his beautiful face. Before she can yell, his mouth bites into hers. He slips the keys back into his pocket.

The sun beats down gloriously, tanning her young body. The tops of her firm breasts glisten with suntan oil, her nipples brush against the wet fabric of her bathing suit. She can't wait until her father leaves the village to go back to the city and she is free to wander the beach on her own. Maybe she'll even peel off her bathing suit top, like those girls from Sweden and France, so that the sun can kiss her young breasts, so that the surf can tickle them gently. As she lies on her stomach, she watches the young man whose towel keeps moving closer to hers. She smiles at him and he smiles back. If only her father would hurry up and leave. But he just sits there, reading his paper. He hasn't said a word to her all day. Some bonding experience this has turned out to be. He's easier to take when he's not interested in her at all. When a phone call on her birthday is too much to ask. At least in their mutual indifference, they don't have to pretend.

She tells him she's taking a swim and he grumbles from behind his paper. The kind of sound a hog makes when it snores. She takes that as an okay, and sashays towards the water. She knows the young man is watching her sway. She can feel it in the dimples on her back. She doesn't even have to look. She enters the sea slowly, like a nymph stepping into sacred water. She floats on her back, lifting her pelvis towards the surface, letting the slow rolling waves carry her deeper and deeper. Her ears fill with water and she can hear the even beat of her heart as her chest rises above the surface, then sinks below, rises and sinks. She hears muted splashing sounds and a body glides underneath hers, then cracks the surface of the water like a dolphin. It is the young man from the beach and he's smiling a big, beautiful smile at her. White, perfect teeth surrounded by soft, full lips. There are drops of sea water sparkling on his eyelashes that make it look as if light is flashing out of his eyes. His jaw bone has been carved by the finest sculptor's tools, and his hair reflects the sun in its tangled, golden tresses. Zeus has come down upon her, or Theseus, or Pericles. He reaches under her and cradles her body in the water, rocking her back and forth in his arms to the rhythm of the waves. He asks for her name, and he tells her his. It is a godly name. She agrees to meet him later that evening in the village square. She will be with her relatives, she warns, but somehow she will escape them. He suggests that they take a walk on the beach. The moon will be full tonight, magical. She smiles and nods in agreement.

They swim off in different directions, emerge from the water a few meters away from each other. Her father is standing, his hand pressed to his forehead for shade. He is waving her over because he is ready to leave. To deposit her with the relatives she doesn't know in the small white house by the sea, and to relieve himself of her keep for a few days.

She doesn't turn back to look at the young man, afraid that he was a figment of her imagination. Too divine to be real. She will look for him later on amongst the crowds in the square. And if she doesn't see him, it will be fine. She will be content to remember him as an enchanted dream, the breath of the gods that blew over her on this sun-drenched, perfect day.

Some Distinguishing Mark

I MET HIM AT AN ART SHOW, one of those affairs you
go to because you have nothing better to do. (It always
starts out innocently like that, nothing you're looking
for—sort of like a venereal disease.) I paced the length of the
gallery, nibbling stale crackers slathered with mildly rancid
brie and sipping cheap white wine out of a plastic goblet,
bored, in search of someone interesting to talk to or look at.
People were clustered in front of the artwork in discreet,
monochromatic sets and, finding no openings, I drained my
goblet and decided to leave. I was on my way out the door
when I spotted him and the ground shifted. What was on the
walls of that gallery, I couldn't say. The moment I laid eyes
on him, I was transported out of that room and into a series
of religious paintings where he had a glowing light coming
out of his head, and I lay scantily clad at his feet in devotion.

He was tall as a hero, with an impish grin. His nose crinkled
when he smiled, and his squinted eyes burned holes into
whatever he fixed them upon. I walked around the room
feeling the edges of the holes with my fingertips, then sat in
a corner behind a salt-white pillar and stared at him for over

an hour. When I ran my knuckles over my face and discovered a hole in my left cheek, I took it as a sign.

Before my brain registered that I'd moved across the room, I was standing in front of him and touching his arm to let him know I wanted him. Wanted him so badly that I couldn't speak. I opened my mouth and nothing, absolutely nothing came out. Shifting my weight from foot to foot, I prayed that divine intervention would push this thing forward, or that he'd do or say something because I knew, deep in the core of my being, that if we did not connect right now, life as I knew it could not proceed. My mouth began to flap on its own, and when my brain finally snapped back into place like a thick rubber band, I found myself smack in the middle of an awkward conversation about mutual acquaintances and the art on the walls that I hadn't looked at—nothing about the light coming out of his head.

He said he was a sculptor and that he built small, violent objects that no one could touch: razor blade sponges and door knockers made of rusty nails and hangers. His studio was around the corner from my apartment. Another sign. I gave him my phone number, but he didn't call. I called him, but he didn't answer. I left baskets of fruit at his studio door —hollowed-out apples stuffed with condoms bearing love notes—and I looked for him on the street like a lost child at the zoo. We met again, by accident, in the cat food aisle at the corner store. He said he saw me go in and found himself following me. He then placed his hand on my breast.

That was the first night he left me to go back to his wife. Left me lying on the kitchen floor amidst broken tumblers of dark rum, the slivers of glass spread around my head, catching moonlight like a halo.

✧ ✧ ✧

There should be some distinguishing mark, like an x tattooed over an eyelid, or a brand on the skin between the nose and cheek—somewhere that can't be hidden, where hair doesn't grow. This would act as a harbinger, an unequivocal warning to turn tail and run before your marbles are spilled over some chiseler who belongs to someone else. And if you ignore the signs, you deserve whatever you get.

I met his wife in a dream a few nights later. Short and pug-faced, she came towards me naked and leaped onto my bed, crushing me beneath her weight like an elephant seal on a far-off beach. She wrestled my hands behind my back and spat into my mouth as she called me a whore, parasite, trash. She then fucked me, raging, banging his cock into me and screaming, "Now you know who's queen, now you know, whore." Of course I knew. She who owns his cock and its deposits is the queen. She who touches it in secret corners and gets her stomach sprayed by it is the whore. The distinction is clear. But every whore wants to usurp the queen and wear the crown jewels in public. What I wore were the bruises she left—blue-green welts and black bite marks that had to be explained to him as the passion of another man, that made him jealous and a little bit rougher. He never would have believed the truth.

I suppose I should've given up on him when the second child was born. Instead, I got pissed off that he still wouldn't put his cock into me but was obviously implanting it into "the long-term deposit," as he called his wife, even though she had stopped washing his come-encrusted jeans. He told me that she accused him of having another life that he kept from her, but she wouldn't leave. What type of woman smells the sweat of another on her husband's balls and doesn't leave? I despised her.

I pictured her waiting for him late into the night, smoking cigarettes and burning holes into their wedding pictures, then flushing the ashes down the toilet. She should have read the signs. When he smashed their wedding gifts in front of the guests, and then passed out on the front lawn cursing her, she could have left. No one would have blamed her, except for their first child, asleep in her belly.

Like an impudent rodent, she became even bolder as time went by, appearing to me while he was still there, wedging herself between her husband's body and mine while we ground into each other. She blocked my cunt with her fist, blew cold air onto her husband's cock until it shrunk into itself. He blamed me for his impotence, and I accepted. After he left, I fought off sleep with caffeine and willpower until it finally pinned me down and knocked me out, and she would be waiting, sitting on the edge of my bed, smoking a cigarette, and smiling wickedly. She no longer found it necessary to catch me off guard, pouncing like a hungry beast. She developed a taste for slow torture—painfully measured movements that made me shudder in anticipation of my punishment.

I hung garlic from my ceiling fan and littered my floor with crucifixes, thumbtacks, and mousetraps. I crawled under my covers clasping a big stick. My dream-self armed herself with guns, large black dogs, and surly bodyguards in fur hats, but they all crumbled into dust and blew away as she reached out to shackle me to the bedposts. She ripped into me until I bled, but I wouldn't give in. This would be a fight to the death.

I started inviting him to parties in distant neighbourhoods to make love. We'd sniff out the nearest bedroom and lock ourselves in, rubbing against each other on piles of coats. We were casting a spell on the coats, I said, which would infuse their owners with the uncontrollable urge to kiss someone they had always desired. It was our service to the world in thanks for our passion. What I didn't admit was that I needed an alternate world, one which denied the emptiness of my bed, the fullness of his, and that in the sanctuary of stranger's homes, I was momentarily safe.

On a cold, windy day, he took me to a terrace by the lake. He looked out towards the horizon and almost floated away. He squeezed my hand, then suggested we fake our suicides and escape on a seafaring vessel to a land where there was no past. Half of me believed him and wanted to go, but there was room for him in my past, in my present, and I already felt dead.

I began to look for her on the streets, staring into the eyes of women pushing prams, brushing up close enough to smell their skin, certain that I would recognize the spicy smell of her perspiration, the residue that was left on my body in the morning, that trailed him like a spectre every time he entered my bedroom. I spent an entire afternoon sitting on a park bench across the street from their apartment building, staring at the door and the windows, willing her to appear. I wanted to see her face in the flesh, to run my fingers over the cicatrices and read the patterns like Braille. I wanted to come to an agreement that appeased her and absolved me of my guilt. I wanted her to stop hurting me, to stop leaving marks. I thought we might strike some sort of bargain.

I slipped into a phone booth around the corner from their building and looked up their number, dropped a coin into the slot, but could not bring myself to dial. I was afraid of the fury I might bring onto myself. Or that her voice would echo in my ears day and night, that its shrillness would follow me around, castigating me until I surrendered. I scratched the number into my palm with a pencil, but by the time I got home, it had disappeared.

One night, while he walked the limbo between me and her, I picked up the phone and her voice entered me before I realized that I had dialed. She answered quickly, as if she'd been expecting me. My heart pounded in my ears, and I was sure she could hear it.

"It's you," she whispered before I could speak, her voice betraying no surprise. "It's about time."

"He's on his way home," I offered nervously. "I'll get to the point. I want you to stop."

"I want *you* to stop," her voice was calm, measured. "You stop and I'll stop."

"It's not that simple."

"I think we should meet."

We agreed to meet the next day at the Motel Sahara, down by the lake. Room number three, three o'clock. She'd make the reservation. She hung up just as I heard him call her name—his disembodied voice echoing from within the black hole he disappeared into when he left me, the imagined place which didn't truly exist until this moment. That night, she did not come.

In the morning, I armed myself with weapons and bribes—a small rubber whip jangled at the bottom of my bag along with a pouch of polished, coloured stones, and a gold coin on a leather thong. I wore an identical coin around my wrist for luck. Somehow I'd decided that if I married her, too, everything would fall into place. At the last moment, I placed two chocolate-dipped cherries in my pocket; a quick antidote if things turned sour.

I walked along the lakeshore towards the motel in a daze, breathing in the smells of rank water and poisoned, dead fish. The horns of cars and trucks from the highway blared distantly, as if in a dream, and one moment I was far away from the motel, the next I was turning the knob on room three, and my eyes met hers for the first time in the daylight.

She was seated at the edge of a king-sized bed, a bed so huge it dwarfed the room it stood in. A baby suckled at her breast, the same baby that should have made me run from him months ago. She looked up at me coolly, and with a nod motioned me to sit down on the bed. I stared at the face I had seen so many times in my dreams, and marvelled over how well I already knew it—the arabesque of small scars by her left nostril, the beauty mark at the outer corner of her right eye. In the daylight, with her blonde hair tied back, wearing a plain green dress, and with her son slurping at her breast, she wasn't so frightening. A sense of relief washed over me, and I was almost happy to see her, as if she and I were old friends about to kiss and make up over some trifle neither of us remembered.

"You're skinnier in person than in the dreams," she began, as she laid the baby to sleep in a basket. "And your skin's not as good."

"Tension," I replied, "makes me break out." I felt my cheeks blushing hot.

"You're not his usual type, you know," she continued, looking me over as if I were a work of art. "He usually likes them petite, reddish, with pointy noses. Sort of like little red-headed ferrets. You're more like a panther. More my type. And you're stronger than the rest. That's why you haven't gone away yet."

I reached into my pocket and offered her a cherry, dangling it before her eyes as if to hypnotize her. She stuck out her tongue and drew it into her mouth like a lizard, turning it around and sucking off the chocolate. I placed the second one in my mouth and bit into it, releasing the liqueur in a quick spurt, hoping for an instant fix. But it was her smell that intoxicated me, that familiar spiciness mixed with baby powder and milk. Feeling faint, I moved to the opposite side of the room and planted myself deep into an overstuffed, orange armchair. She followed me, letting her dress slide to the floor. My heart banged against my ribs like a fist as she sat on my lap facing me, her breasts resting on my collarbone.

"If you're his, you're mine. That's what wedding vows are for." She pushed my face into her cleavage, then stroked my hair while unzipping my blouse and unhinging my bra. My sleeves slid off my shoulders, and she looked shocked as she noticed the bruises. She began kissing and licking them, desperately apologizing as if I was one of her babies who she'd slapped in a moment of anger. She then took me by the elbow and led me to the gigantic bed. She lay down on top of me and shut her eyes. A tear spilled into my mouth, then another, and another. We lay there all afternoon, barely moving, as I drank her tears like mother's milk, the baby cooing from the corner like a dove in his sleep.

When the shadows of sunset fell upon the dirty brown rug and it was time to go, I kissed her eyelids and her mouth, and then slipped the gold coin around her neck. It caught the last ray of sunlight shining between her milk-heavy breasts. I kissed the soft brown nipples and a faint trace of milk rubbed onto my lips. We left the motel, holding the baby-basket between us, while overweight businessmen and their cheap, high-heeled secretaries turned away from us in shame.

Later that evening was the last time he and I were alone together, but I was no longer present. I had already been pulled into that hollow pit in my stomach where I anticipated his departure from the moment he arrived. And now that I knew where he was going, I hated him for his privilege and could no longer participate or pretend. He kissed my mouth and, out of habit, it kissed him back. He must have tasted my absence on my tongue, between my legs, because he slid into me for the first time, his cock peering around corners to find me. When I did not reappear, he went home to her, and I came back out and cried.

That same night she visited my dreams, but she was transformed, no longer a nightmare. She looked tired and worn, as if she'd been up all night comforting crying children. I held out the blankets, inviting her in. She snuggled up beside me and I cradled her head and stroked her blonde curls. I climbed on top of her and kissed her eyelids and mouth, then slipped his cock into her. I thrust slowly and gently until she was quietly gasping for air. She held on to my hip bones and lifted herself up towards me until she came. Then we slept, but in the morning my legs were wrapped around my pillow and she was gone. And that was the end.

It turned out that he was the one who wouldn't leave her—too comfortable with the routine, too afraid of the unknown. The word on the street is that she threw him out and took up with another woman. He did the same. Neither of them is me.

I saw him with his new girlfriend today, a skinny woman with bad teeth and dyed red hair, ferret-like and too young. I told him that I was leaving town, escaping the past. He said the signs were there all the time and he wished me good luck. When he shook my hand, a glint of yellow light glanced across his face and he noticed the gold coin on a thong wrapped around my wrist. He stared at the coin for a moment, then stuffed his hands in his pockets and looked away. His girlfriend looked at me curiously, then at him, and her smile evaporated, as if she suddenly saw a welt rise from his cheek, a marking, invisible until now, that would never disappear again.

HORACE LIKES DEMONS

HORACE LIKES DEMONS. He brings them home all the time because he likes the way they laugh—heads thrown back, voices bellowing towards the ceiling—with no sign of self-consciousness or restraint. He also enjoys watching demons chew tobacco with their mouths open. They slide the black chunk past yellow teeth, then spew sticky morsels out the window at little old ladies who pretend nothing has hit them, but run home on geriatric limbs to rinse the tobacco stains out with soda water and salt. Horace has taken to practicing his aim at home, and all the soda water and salt on the planet could not remove the brown speckles of tobacco juice that spot our apartment. But there's no stopping Horace. He doesn't respond to reason.

Horace lives inside of me. He is my *doppelganger*, my worst half, the devil in my ear. He is my self-fulfilled prophecy of doom. The reason I have so many gaping wounds. Without a second thought, Horace trades me off for his own amusement to murderers, cads, and pigdogs with needles in their pockets and knives in their boots. Delectable, unreliable assholes. And when I come to, I find myself in bed with a demon.

Demons are unconcerned with the proprieties of everyday life. They curse store clerks unfortunate enough to have run out of their brand of triple X whiskey, threatening them with the fire and brimstone of hell. They tweak the buttocks of prepubescent schoolgirls as they skip home from school, then howl and slap each other's backs when the girls start to cry. They recognize each other through complex hand-signals and eye movements, like the members of a secret society. They are always looking for new recruits. They are always looking for food. They hold meetings on nights when the moon is swamped by fog, and cold drizzle pierces through to the bone. Horace cannot stay away.

When I try to keep Horace at home, the demons come after him. They serenade him with the cries of mating cats, make kissing noises outside our window until he is bouncing off the walls, clawing at the furniture, and rubbing himself up against my leg. He wants to go so badly that he whimpers inconsolably if he cannot. Sometimes this is even worse. It wears me down, so I let him out, though I'm compelled to trail close behind.

At the meetings the demons dance around in circles, arms draped over shoulders. They trip each other and laugh as they help their fallen comrades up off the floor, only to trip them again. They drink and smoke and piss in pots in the corner. They kiss each other on the mouth and then pretend it didn't happen. Some eat roast pork, while others swear by vegetables, but they all eat with their hands and then toss the remains into the air with wild abandon. In the morning, women are brought in to deal with the mess because demons never stick around to clean up.

The most important aspect of the meeting, and the most solemn, is the information exchange. The demons trade passwords and pass keys along with information about who can be unlocked by what means. Names, addresses, tastes, and smells are memorized, recorded indelibly on the demons' brains for easy reference. This is what demons live for: the hunt, the plunder, the feed.

Horace comes home singing and bumping into things after a night out with the fellows. I toss him into bed without washing his face, and he falls into a fitful, blissful sleep. In the morning, I'm the one who has to deal with the mess.

Horace has introduced me to all of his comrades. Or rather, they come to me because they know I am with him. I am marked. They strike a bargain with Horace while I'm in the washroom, and when I come back out I am bound hand and foot by their complicity.

It's an odd threesome, sometimes even fun, though I can't help but think that they are having the better time, pulling at each other's cocks and making faces at me after I'm tied to the bed and blindfolded. I've heard the snickering more than once. Horace is the smart one, though. He does his damage and then goes to sleep in some unknown place, so when morning comes, I'm the one who has to make the demon breakfast, who has to push him out the door while making sure he hasn't made off with any part of me. They do that, demons. They're stealers. Count your fingers, count your toes, lift your hands up to your nose, do you still have one of those? Ask the demon what he knows. I made that up as a sort of easy inventory to check whether I'm intact before I shut the door. Often, I'm not. But how do you get back a thing that's already been eaten?

I must admit that there's something very attractive about those demons, something about their squinty eyes and sardonic grins that does turn my head. I can't help it. It's like there's a switch inside me just waiting to be flicked. And Horace encourages me, whispers dirty limericks into my ear, and before I know it, he is pushing me across the street into oncoming traffic, pressing me up against the demon *du jour*, giving him my phone number.

Then I sit at home and agonize. Will he call? Was it real? And lately, so what's the catch? What part of me has Horace sold for his own gain?

Stop it, Horace. You're hurting me.

Don't get me wrong; I like Horace. He can be a one-man Mardi Gras if he's in the right mood. But he has no conscience and very little memory. He doesn't remember the bruises his friends leave on my arms when they shake me in anger in the middle of the night, not even when we inspect them together in the morning. He is always apologetic and promises to take better care of me, to choose more prudently, to be gentler. But then he forgets again and, when night falls, I find myself wrestling with some new demon. Sometimes I instigate these fights, certain I can win, but I can't. I don't have the drive Horace has, the passion for self-fulfillment, the dedication to my own pleasure. Nothing else figures in his calculation. You could say he is the ultimate hedonist, or perhaps a charming sociopath, raping and pillaging with a rose between his teeth, indulging without a second thought. That's all nice and fine in a storybook character, but who wants to live with him? I live with him. I've tried to throw him out, but I can't. I've tried to smother him in the middle of the night with a feather pillow, but I'm the one whose breath becomes short, who begins to black out, to die. We are inseparable. The best I can do is cope, strategize, try not give in to his smile. I don't always succeed.

I don't know when Horace was born, perhaps on the same day as me, but he has led an entirely different life. It must be incredible not to have a body that bruises, to be incarnate and immaterial at the same time. When Horace's whims finally kill me, my ghost will impregnate some unsuspecting soul with *my* desire, and I will then assert my power, my will, just to see what it feels like. I'll hide in a cave in the body's heart and squeeze until the wretch thinks his chest is going to explode. I'll choose his lovers and make him betray them. I'll blaspheme in front of his mother and let loose the worst family secret. I'll smirk as he agonizes over what is happening to him, as he wonders out loud whether some succubus has entered his veins and is forcing him to retrace the same futile path, to crave that which will lead to his ultimate destruction. I'm sure it's more satisfying that way, if the victim struggles, puts up a valiant fight, but nevertheless falls to his knees, surrenders to his addiction, to my appetite. Where is the story in someone submitting to your will unquestioningly? I'm sure we will laugh heartily at the meetings.

The best revenge would be to turn on Horace. To chain him to the bathroom sink and lock the door. To blast music in his ears so he is deafened, and light matches under his feet to keep him dancing in the little circle the leash allows. He won't be able to hear the cat calls of his demon friends beneath the windows. He won't be able to drag me out the door with him by the crucifix I wear around my waist.

I do not enjoy the prospect of dismantling his spirit, but there is no middle ground with a type like Horace; he's into extremes. Pleasure/Pain. Love/Obsession. He thrives on danger and walks the line between fantastical joy and utter catastrophe. I've got to find something for him to do soon, put his talents to good use before they kill me; before I kill him. After all, he is quite the character. How many men do you know who can laugh and weep at the same time?

I met someone today, while Horace was asleep. Julius—a cute

blond with a halo, a whittling knife, and an armload of flowers. Not a blemish on his skin, not a mean bone in his body. He entered me at the cemetery while I was picking out a plot. Julius is going to run things for a spell, just so I can see how he does. Horace is being replaced; he doesn't know yet. Ssshhh.

It wasn't easy or pleasant getting the duct-tape over Horace's mouth, but his screams were killing dogs, waking the neighbours. And when he begged and winked and promised, I got weak in the knees. He's so much more manageable tied to that chair, though it makes me sad to see him there, and I still want him. My hope is that with time I'll be able to untie him, see the error of his ways, stop finding him exciting. I've brought in a specialist once a week, a demonologist with big, fleshy hands, which she lays on my forehead while mumbling incantations under her breath. She works with both of us, like a marriage counsellor. My task is to stop giving in; his is to find some sort of lesser torture to keep himself occupied —one that does not involve my flesh. He is not co-operating. It is all up to me.

I came up with the idea that Horace might like to draw in his spare time; perhaps write a play or some poetry. Those are the types of things he'd be best at. Witty repartee, flawless illusion. That commitment to the perfect moment. I bought him pens and stacks of coloured paper, but he won't touch them. He just growls when I walk by. His main grievance is that I am throwing out everything he's worked for all these years. All the magical contributions he's made to my life, those flights of fancy that have allowed us to transcend the mundane. He needn't worry; I'm not throwing anything out. I'm life's perfect pack rat. I write everything down. There will always be a place for him in my heart because in some areas he has exquisite taste and will definitely be consulted: restaurants, operas, haircuts, perfumes. And he tells a damn fine story. But no choosing men, absolutely not. I feel guilty. We've been together a long time. I offer him an orchid, but he tears it open with his teeth and spits the petals in my face. Crows Julius' name as if it were a disease. I am hurt. And unsure.

I try to explain one last time that I love him, I truly do, but that Julius has a different approach, a lighter touch, less addictive. He stops to smell the flowers, and I want to smell the flowers. I like flowers. I pick up the scattered petals and eat them one by one. When I am finished, Horace has vanished, melted into the chair. I lock it in the attic, but I know better. Horace is uncontainable. Every morning when I wake up, I brace myself against him, say a little prayer, exorcise my inner demons and hope for the best. Sometimes, when I get comfortable, let my guard down, Horace jumps on my back and spins me around until my heart is dizzy. Until I don't know where I am, what hit me, what I'm doing, or who I'm talking to—except that he's a demon. So tasty. And I'm hungry, so hungry for that meal Horace prepares best. Momentarily I am ready to follow him anywhere. Horace smiles and licks his fingers one at a time, then turns me around so I can see the tour bus barreling down in my direction. He dives into my chest, laughing, just as some demon grabs my arm and tries to hold me in place. From the sidewalk, I see a busload of travelling priests and nuns holding rosaries to the window, crossing themselves fervently and beseeching their God.

I run home, take a deep breath, and repeat my vows to Julius. What a nice guy, that Julius. Not one bruise since I brought him in, and the dishes are always done. It's a good life, I guess. Not very exciting, but a good life. Ssshhh. Julius is asleep, and I have this moment to myself.

Sometimes, at night, after I've pulled down the blinds and crawled into bed with Julius, I can't help wondering whether Horace was right for me. Whether this daily fight against him is more damaging than a hundred Horaces going down on me in relentless succession, flying away with chunks of skin, blood, heart, vulva. Whether it's worth locking myself in my room, turning off the phone, plugging my ears against the mating cat serenades—just for the sake of remaining safe. I am not always up for the fight against that which I crave. I guess I'm just a masochist, a volunteer victim. Or maybe this is my demon talking. The voice of a woman possessed. Just call me Horace.

DEAR MR. BAIL

"There has been a mistake—but of no great importance—made in the denomination of this picture. The woman depicted is not 'The Drover's Wife.' She is my wife. We have not seen each other now . . . it must be getting on thirty years."
                    —MURRAY BAIL, *The Drover's Wife*

DEAR MR. BAIL,
   I would like to report that I found the Drover's wife lying face down in a puddle on the street, here in Toronto. This was on College Street, to be exact, in Little Italy. I don't know whether she tried to get directions back to Australia, but with the glut of Italians in the neighbourhood, she probably had a hard time communicating. And they, I'm sure, had a hard time understanding her accent. They are not unfriendly here in Little Italy, just suspicious of strangers.

   How she got into the street, and who was the first to run her over, I don't know. But her skirt was up over her hips and there were tire tracks criss-crossing her back, not a pretty sight. Okay, I admit I ran her over, too. But just with my bike, and at least I stopped. Okay, not immediately. I got to the sidewalk and then turned back. I looked around to see if anyone else might help her, take the responsibility, but all I saw were numb stares and noses grazing the sky or the sidewalk, depending on the degree of ennui and self-esteem.

Yes, I hesitated, but with good reason. You see, I've had a similar experience in the past, at a corner near a church on Carlton Street. A man with the face of petrified, grey horror, who smelled of old socks, festering meat and gin, fell face first into the street. I saw him fall and heard the smack of bone on cement. It was surprisingly loud and distinct, considering traffic, as if everything stood still for a moment. This was the man's standing ovation, and he was missing it.

No one would help me lift him off the pavement. I have been described as small-boned, and he could be described as dead weight, so I couldn't even drag him an inch by myself, let alone lift him. I looked towards a black woman at the bus shelter with that desperate expression reserved for long bathroom lines at the movies, but she recoiled, shaking her head as if I'd asked her to abort Jesus.

Four men with Humpty Dumpty waistlines appeared out of nowhere, as if they'd rehearsed for this moment for weeks, and rolled him over. I looked into the man's face and locked onto his eyes, icy blue. A trickle of blood slithered down his forehead and over his right eyebrow, a red tributary emptying into his eye.

I offered to find a phone, and the rotund men nodded in unison. The phone booths were a right angle away from where I was standing, on the other side of the street, so I went into the church instead. Later, when I went over that choice, closer to the event in question, I concluded that I chose the church because I didn't want to cross at two different intersections (I don't like cars, they scare me). But now, in writing this letter, I realize that I chose the church because somewhere, deep down in my heathen psyche, the archetype for God still resides, and as an extension (like bungalows), the recognition of priests as caring, and the house of God as a safe and charitable haven open to all who need help. The right place to go and yell in a voice loud and desperate, tinged with a Southern accent, "Father, there's an angel fallen in the streets, come quickly." The priest would look at me in a combination of pained disbelief and alarm, realizing that his moment had come. That the big test they'd prepared him for at the seminary, that he'd prepared himself for since childhood through devotion, fasting, meditation, and abstinence from sex was finally here. And this was the day that, if he were good enough, he'd get his wings.

Of course my priest didn't have wings, just Hush Puppies and a limp. He wasn't even on the shortlist for wings. I explained that a man had fallen in the street, face first, crunch, using sophisticated hand gestures to demonstrate precisely the occurrence and my point, which was that he should call an ambulance immediately because the man didn't look like he had long for this earth, and his audience was starting to thin.

The priest stared at me blankly and then consulted Igor, the overgrown altar boy (they have push buttons for bell tolling in this church, but they sound like synthesizers, weak and hollow, as if they've been castrated). They both looked me over at the same time: first my rumpled hat, then my boots, their gaze finally resting on my naked knee peeking out of my torn jeans. "Show me where," the priest said, leading the way down the hall. I did not mention the doctrine he swears by that requires him to believe in exactly that which he does not see. I just followed his sticky brown shoes down the hall. Igor followed at a skittish pace, like those seabirds at Biloxi Beach in Mississippi that move like overgrown gnats with feathers.

When we got to the front door and opened it towards the light, the whole scene had disappeared, including the victim, the rotund men, and the black Virgin Mary. The priest and Igor scowled at me, then pushed me down the stairs. The priest wiped his hands clean of me with that rhythmic, clapping back and forth dance step motion, which also turns old people's lights on and off. Igor spat his bubble gum in my general direction, and then they disappeared inside, slamming the heavy door behind them, leaving me sprawled on my butt on the sidewalk. I looked around for the Humpty Dumpty men, but I guess they had already gone home to celebrate the arrival of their big moment, so I got up, dusted myself off, and left.

The bad thing about that happening, and all other happenings, is that it began to fade once the objects of the happening were taken away. It shrank like a dream, until there is no way left to prove it even happened. Unless someone took a picture, and even that might not help. Everything eventually disappears.

Imagine an old woman rocking back and forth, muttering to herself in the cramped attic where she's been relegated along with boxes of old clothes, broken furniture, and mouldy stacks of newspapers. Everything she owned, all the objects that defined her existence—her religious icons, her orange straw sewing basket, her mink hat—have been given away to charity, or plundered by greedy relatives. She has fallen out of context, and no one has much use for her anymore, though they sometimes reminisce about the pies she used to bake and smack their lips. She sits up there alone in the near-dark, rummaging through a box of family photos. She smiles at the children in sailor suits and cowboy hats, at the charming young bride with her handsome groom. Her eyes glaze over as she stares at the elegant blue script that covers the yellowed pages of her diary. She tears the brittle pages into tiny pieces and eats them, then disposes of the photos in the same manner. She grins at me when I bring up her dinner, shreds of memory poking out between her teeth like feathers. She bites my fingers when I try to pluck them out.

The rest of her family does not understand; they are annoyed and resentful and sigh harshly at her every coo. You see, Mr. Bail, they have been counting on her as the repository of their life, the place where they can be the protagonist whenever they feel unappreciated by the rest of the world. How dare she forget? They quiz her for the whole thirty minutes of their quarterly visit, and she isn't pretending, she truly can't answer any of their questions. "Come now, don't you remember me? It's Pete, Auntie. Peter. Remember how you used to tie me to the sofa leg so I wouldn't break your porcelain figurines, Auntie?" She isn't even sure who the people asking the questions are, or what some of the words mean. So she starts talking to mirrors instead of people because people make her feel crazy with all of their questions, expectations, and condescending smiles. She goes to the mirror to ask it what she still knows, and before it can answer, these strangers have put her, for her own good, into an institution with white walls, puréed green food, plenty of mirrors, and no taboo about talking into them. "Mirror, mirror on the wall, did I ever exist at all?"

There are three mirrors in her room, side by side, positioned so she can even talk to the back of her head. She can see three images of herself at once and gives each one a different name. On some days she knows all three, though the middle one won't stop crying, the one on the right is either Lucy or

Catherine depending on the weather, and she's not on speaking terms with the one on the left, though they grimace at each other from time to time and then turn their backs.

One day they hatch a plan, and she escapes with the other three hiding under her coat. Once outside, she directs them to spread out, "'Cause they can't take all of us at the same time." She wanders the streets of Toronto on her own, wearing a trenchcoat, a blue hospital gown, and paper slippers soggy with rain and dirt. She tugs on her crazy hair, mutters to herself, and screams in a language that only she and her cohorts understand. People on the sidewalk veer around her, afraid that they'll catch whatever it is she has. Old age, senility, insanity, uselessness—they aren't sure what. "Where did you come from, where do you live?" a young policeman asks, but she just grabs his face with her hands, hisses in his ear like a deflating balloon, and laughs. Tells him she loves him and kisses him on his thin, bloodless lips. She then spots Lucy out of the corner of her eye and runs across the street to give her a bus ticket, since she knows Lucy's off to visit her daughter to make her miserable. And she gets hit by a car just when she's about to reach her. She didn't check the traffic lights because she doesn't remember anything like that ever existed, let alone that there is some use for such a thing other than pretty flashing lights to dance to. Memories of such things are without importance in the institution. As unimportant as the fact that she's forgotten her name.

I go by that corner and that church every once in a while. I stare at that piece of pavement, and for the time being, the fallen man always reappears. Maybe I should have brought him home with me, too. Maybe I did.

I don't stop much anymore except to toss a quarter to a musician, or a dollar to the older men who look as if they might be someone's grandfather who escaped from the circus wearing red-striped flood pants and a gangly purple sweater. There's no more room left in my apartment. I even have to do all my writing at my kitchen table. But they still follow me, on the streets, down hallways, to the elevator, pleading with me to take them home, clawing at the doors until their fingers bleed, until the nurse takes them back to their beds and straps them down. I can see them, even with my back turned. And then I cry. There just isn't enough room.

So as you can see, Mr. Bail, I have very good reasons for hesitating when I see someone laying face first on the street. I need some time to work out my dilemma. Should I bother at all with a good deed since no memory of it will comfort me in my old age? Or is it like Vladimir said in *Waiting for Godot*: "Let us do something while we have the chance. It is not every day that we are needed." I usually opt for the latter, to remain in the present, to do my share, and that's how I came to pick up the Drover's wife. I wiped the rain off her with my sleeve, smoothed down her hair, then perched her on the back of my bike and brought her home with me.

Though a little crumpled and warped, and starting to show her age around the edges, she's happy here with me. We drink raspberry tea in the afternoons and ride the streetcar back and forth without a destination to eavesdrop on other lives. Mostly they're boring, but every once in a while we hear a gem and write it down in a small black and red notebook. I don't think the scars across her back will ever really heal, though they did prove to be an interesting conversation piece at a recent cocktail party where I dared her to wear a backless cocktail dress, and she did. She's still feisty, for all the wear and tear.

She says she likes it here because no one asks her any

questions about her past. As for me, I only know her as she is now, and have never been to Australia, so she can tell me anything she wants and I'll believe her. I think I'm even beginning to pick up a bit of her accent, as well as a few strange words that she may or may not have made up. This has caused some eye-rolling in the neighbourhood, but I never attempt to explain. Most people don't recognize truth when they hear it, so what harm could a few made-up words do to my vocabulary, anyway? When they do ask, I tell them I'm speaking in tongues.

Before I forget, a message to the Drover: stop searching for her. She doesn't look like her picture anymore. I've cut her hair into a "bob" and have given her a pair of my cat's eye sunglasses. She's considered quite eccentric in the neighbourhood, and she enjoys that. She's not coming back. She doesn't even remember that she had a husband, and I think it's best for all concerned that it stays that way. If it weren't for my chancing upon your report, Mr. Bail, I wouldn't even know what a Drover was. She didn't look very happy in the picture. She answers to Peggy here in Toronto, and laughs whenever she hears me call her by name. She thinks it's a funny name, one you'd give to a cow. I've grown used to her and can't imagine living without her now that we've found each other. (Do you believe in karma? I do.) I need her here. She has been an inspiration and a comfort.

Mr. Bail, I leave the decision of whether to pass this information on to the proper authorities up to you. I just thought you'd be interested in her whereabouts. Yours was the only name in her shirt pocket.

(Inspired by the discovery of Murray Bail's book, The Drover's Wife, *on the wet and indifferent streets of Toronto.)*

How to
Pick Up Women

I'VE NEVER SEEN YOU HERE before," the halter-topped beauty says, flashing a blinding smile in the over-crowded bar. I am bathed in light she casts, as if angels have chosen me for a heavenly mission. She stretches her hand towards my face and strokes away a loose strand of hair that has fallen into my eyes. My gaze slides down the dark skin of her arm, shiny with sweat, and my nostrils pucker. She smells like oranges and mangos. I want to bite into her and let her sweet juices slide down my chin and trickle over my breasts. She leans closer and purrs, then softly blows into my ear as if to erase any second thoughts that might be creeping in.

"Second time," I manage. "Only my second . . . second time."

My arms swing limply by my sides while she strums her fingers along the back of my neck. Her cheek presses to mine, and her lips flutter against my ear as she tells me about herself. Her thumbs have already traced my torso, hooked the belt loops of my jeans.

I nod to the rhythm and inflection of her voice. The rise and fall of her chest holds me in near hypnosis. She does not allow me a word in edgewise, and even though I am now fully mesmerized by the subtle movements that have allowed her to run her fingers all over my body, I oscillate between two distinct thoughts: "She's so self-centred, she could be a man," swinging up against, "How appropriate would it be for me to slide my hand into the side of her halter top, where the fabric gathers by her left breast, so I could caress the pointed nipple that keeps brushing up against my arm?" I look around. No one else is burying hands in halter tops, so I figure this is probably not conventional etiquette in here.

I try to follow her sign language, but cannot make out the gestures. I need a phrasebook, a map, a train schedule. A paralysis spreads throughout my body, and I'm afraid even to lift a finger in case the gesture translates into something obscene or completely obtuse that will give me away. She unhinges herself from my belt loops and moves away just as my hands begin to rise. Her tongue glides across her lips, and her monologue comes to an abrupt end.

"Gotta go, my friends are waiting. It's been pish."

What does that mean? What language, and where do I sign up for classes? I wish I had applied myself when I was younger. You pick up things much quicker when you're young. Not even a kiss goodbye.

In another club, when I was younger, Rodrigo leaned me up against the back wall by the cigarette machine. With light-ning-quick movements, he slid one hand down my pants, slithered the other up my shirt, past the underwire of my bra, twisting my left nipple between thumb and forefinger. His fingers worked expertly as if he were tuning a short-wave radio. Every once in a while he would hit a foreign frequency, and only his tongue filling my mouth kept me from singing out loud in German, Romanian, Basque. That was the summer I became multilingual.

A woman leaning against the cigarette machine comes up to me and asks if I want to dance. I look at her and decide she's not my type. Not that I have a type when it comes to women, but somehow I know she's not it. Shorn hair and big pants; I'm surprised she likes me. I shake my head and shrug my shoulders a little, tell her I don't like the song, and fill my mouth with bourbon. I truly am sorry, more sorry than I'd be for a man; I know what it feels like to be a rejected woman. She shrugs, grins sheepishly, and disappears into the crowd.

A song I like comes on. The beginning sounds like that Smiths tune that goes, "I am human and I need to be loved, just like everyone else does." Finally, something I understand. I put down my glass and move towards the dance floor with confidence, elbow out enough space for my arms to weave tapestries in the air. But I have been deceived. The song turns into something else, and I am trapped amidst writhing, happy, female bodies. I stay anyway. I love to dance by myself. I came to the club by myself. I didn't know how else to go about it. I didn't have anyone else to bring along.

I was dancing by myself to a Smiths tune at Bert's party. It was late and people were filing out in bunches, the way that sort of lemming consensus always happens. Bert wasn't my lover yet, but it was in the air, and he had already seen me naked. I swayed in the dim light, my arms slicing through the thickness of innuendo while Bert picked up paper plates soggy with half-eaten celery sticks and dollops of anchovy paste. Bert's ex-girlfriend Mariah came out of the bathroom and asked me to dance. She put her arms around my waist and pulled me towards her. Her slow, even breath in my ear filled my brain with strange, misty images that transformed all the ideas I'd had about Bert into a four-breasted beast. The air shifted, and the scent of pineapples and peaches wafted into the room.

Mariah led me by the hand to her bathtub and her bed. She taught me my first words. I eventually slept with Bert; she recommended it. But we never told him about us. We thought he'd like it too much.

Last call, and groups of women are leaving the club. There is more space to dance, more space to look around and listen. The shorn woman is still staring at me, and I dance with my back to her. A bad disco song comes on, and I go back to the speaker and pick up my drink. My glass is empty except for an ice cube, which I suck on while trying to figure out how to stand. Is my posture around men different? It must be. Standing there looking at the remaining prospects, I am transported to my seventh grade gym class on the day the cool girls caught me with tissues stuffed down my bra. I straighten my back and puff out my chest. I bite down hard on the ice to keep myself in the present.

Men are easier. The slightest hint of interest from a woman and they're wagging their tails, licking her face, and rolling over on their backs for their bellies to be scratched. Women need finesse: a perfectly-timed come-hither look that has a dash of playfulness and a smattering of seduction mixed in; a tone of voice that is flawless, offering both friendliness and promise, while betraying no hint of insecurity. It's because they're women and they know how to do it. As I scan the room one last time, I decide I feel sorry for men.

I spot someone who may be my type. Black leather jacket and a unitard. Good, heavy boots and long, brown hair. A slash of red across her mouth. I like lipstick. It leaves a trail. She's alone at the bar. The last sliver of ice melts into my tongue, and I put down my glass. It trembles on the surface of the speaker. The vibrations slowly push it towards the edge.

I used to play a game with Rodrigo and his girlfriend Darian. We called it piss-kissing. Darian would pour cognac into her mouth and swirl it around until it got really warm. She'd then release it into my mouth in a slow, steady stream, moving in closer as her mouth emptied until our lips almost touched. I would do the same thing to Rodrigo, and he'd then pass it back to her. With every piss-kiss, some liquid would be swallowed. The person who swallowed the last drop had to choose one of the other two for a long, tangled French kiss. I always chose Rodrigo. He always chose Darian. She always chose me. It was very exciting, and they always asked me to go home with them afterwards, but I always refused. My excuse was that my boyfriend, Phil, who didn't like clubs, was expecting me. I'd go to his apartment and fuck him all night long instead. He never asked why.

I often wish I'd gone home with Rodrigo and Darian, at least once. But those feelings I'd get when she smeared her blackberry lip gloss onto my mouth were so strong, so unknown, that I was too scared to unleash them, even in my own head. Imagine how fluent I'd be now.

The strobe light makes me trip on the carpet and I blush. I'm glad that it's dark and she has her back to me. I get a last drink right under the nose of the cut off point. J.D., straight up, for courage, for life, for hair on my chest. I suck it back but leave one drop burning under my tongue, like a crib note. I lick my lips, slide over towards her, and compliment her boots—simply but confidently, with that touch of innuendo. "Nice boots." She looks at me and smiles, a sly smile that vaporizes that last drop of J.D. She glances at my boots and nods approval. Her hair smells of coconut, and I want to plant my lips on the back of her neck and stay there for a long time. "But can they dance," I continue, rather suavely, then lead her towards the dance floor. Another bad disco song gives way to the last dance of the night, a slow dance. How opportune. My arms wrap around her waist, and I breathe and breathe into her ear, hoping that some of my breathing will translate into something she understands, senses, pictures, desires. Her arms wrap around my neck, and I feel her tongue on my earlobe. I've done it. I've learned the language. I've pronounced the words. I've found a train schedule and I can now reach my destination. How pish!

Later, as I drizzle more guava-scented bath oil into my tub, Celeste comments that we look alike. Of course we do, I reply, splashing water on her breasts and kissing her throat. We're both women.

FRAGMENTS OF THE ACROPOLIS

I AM SITTING BY MYSELF in the Rialto Cinema, the Greek theatre on Park Avenue in Montreal. It is Saturday afternoon—Father/Daughter day—and I have been sent to the kiddy matinee once again so that part of the dreaded day can be eaten up by a movie. My other option would be to sit in my father's printing shop and fold newspapers to the clanking rhythm of ancient typesetting machines, or to stamp my name repeatedly on pieces of paper, on walls, on my arms and forehead with the metal stamp he has made up for me to keep me busy. Even at that early age, I like seeing my name in print.

After the movie is over, my father will pick me up and take me to lunch at Dusty's—a dive that is next to the printing shop, though I'm too young to know it's a dive, and I like it. He will then give me some money to buy a comic book. More distraction. I spend what seems like hours in the comic book aisle of the local drugstore—conveniently next to Dusty's. I like to look through the adult comic books at the drawings of humongous-breasted, naked women in compromising cartoon positions. I steal one of these comic books by tucking it into an Archie or Casper the Friendly Ghost comic book. I guiltily smuggle it out of the drugstore so I can study the drawings in the privacy of the printing shop bathroom, but that's a whole other story.

The kiddy matinee today features a movie based on Greek myth. There are heroes with golden shields, there are raven-haired maidens in flowing white tunics and sandals, and there are mythological creatures. One scene takes place at the Acropolis, or some movie set facsimile of the Acropolis, but since this is a flashback, I have to assume that at the tender age of eight I believed, I still believed.

It is nighttime in the scene and the hero and his golden shield move around the marble columns cautiously, as if expecting someone to jump out from behind them for an impromptu swordfight. At least that's what I expect. Instead, six or seven screeching creatures fly down into the Acropolis. They are human in size, but have gargoyle faces and huge bat-like wings. The hero kills a few, and a few others escape. One of the escaping creatures may even carry off a raven-haired maiden in its claws, but I'm not sure whether I saw this or if it is what I most feared.

As I exit the dark theatre into the afternoon light, I hope that next Saturday the matinee will be nothing more menacing than a kung fu movie. My father, waiting outside impatiently, then takes me to lunch, I buy my comic book, and I am eventually sent home to my mother. I don't tell anyone about the creatures. I don't know if I have nightmares about them that night or not.

I am ten years old and in Greece for the first time since my birth. I am driving around with my mother and some man who is either a relative or the reception clerk at the Atlantis Hotel in Athens, where we are staying. It is nighttime and we drive past the Acropolis, which is magically lit up in different colours—red, green, blue—a stately apparition in the night sky. The man asks my mother if she wants to go up to the Parthenon and she is enthusiastic—I, less so. He says he knows a secret way in, since the Acropolis is not open to the public at night. I begin to whine in the back seat, complaining that I am tired and don't want to go. (I imagine I spoiled my single mother's fun more than once in my life.) The man counters that I am missing a rare opportunity to see the Acropolis without anyone else around, not to mention the view of the city. I hold my ground—I'm not interested. I want to go back to the hotel to sleep. We drive away from the Acropolis in silence (there's nothing more frightening to a stranger than a whining little girl he has no authority over), and I'm suddenly not so tired or cranky anymore. I want to go for ice cream, and I want roasted pumpkin seeds in a paper bag from a street vendor. I never let on that my reticence is due to monsters, gargoyles with wings that kidnap raven-haired maidens like me from the Acropolis at night. And the hero can do nothing about it.

In the light of day, when the world is safe from nightmare creatures, my mother and I make the dusty climb up to the Acropolis. I am wearing shorts, a t-shirt, and leather sandals. I am all angles and planes, lanky, spidery. I scramble from structure to structure, running my fingers over the carved marble in awe of the ancientness, then climb the too-high steps and imagine the stretched-out arms and legs of my ancestors. I pose in front of the Parthenon and feel divine.

After all those centuries, there is still marble dust wafting around up there, as if someone in a corner is still carving, still fashioning new statues, new rooms. The soles of my sandals are white with dust, and I announce to my mother that I will never step in a puddle again, now that I have walked where my illustrious, spidery ancestors have walked. The importance of this impressive history is not beyond me at ten. I am completely sucked into the power of ancient Greece.

At the foot of the Parthenon, I pick up a stone and slip it into my pocket. A souvenir piece of history that I smuggle out past the soldiers who are taking down the Greek flag, past the man at the gate who takes the tickets, and the woman at the kiosk who sells the glossy-plated books with photographs of ancient treasures and a fold-out map that shows the Acropolis when it was complete. I ask my mother to buy me one of the books, and she does. That night at the hotel, I place the stone on the map and fall into an enchanted, mythological sleep.

The next year, when I am eleven, I am taken to Crete to meet my father's family. His brother takes me to the Minoan palace of Knossos, but I do not steal a stone, and I step liberally into puddles afterwards. For some reason, I am not as impressed as I was with the Acropolis.

I am a teenager, newly seventeen, and I am being sent to Greece to live with my father, who now lives there. "If you think you've got it bad here with me, go live with your father and we'll see how much you like that!" This is the worst punishment my mother can come up with. She arranges the exchange with him, one of the last times they will actually speak to each other. He gets me at the height of my teenage rebellion; she gets peace and freedom.

At the airport, she recants and tells me that if I am not having a good time, I can come home. I am not a thing to be sent away and brought back at her whim, I decide as I kiss her goodbye. I stay for six months, having a miserable time, to spite her.

But at the beginning of the trip I am in good spirits because my best friend Sabrina, an Italian with whom I share secrets, lies, and most of my time, is coming with me for the first three weeks. Because we are together, when we land in Athens and get into a cab we do not feel the distance we have travelled. We might have just taken an extended bus ride from our Montreal homes to some village or suburb. As we approach Athens, the Acropolis suddenly juts out and smacks both of us on the forehead, and it finally occurs to us that we are far away from the usual. It is only then that we get excited.

The next afternoon, we walk to the Acropolis, and on our way up we are accosted by a con artist who begs us to let him photograph us. Sabrina doesn't want to be photographed, and neither do I, but he insists, and I cave in. Sabrina and I pose for the photograph we don't want, feeling stupid. He then asks for our address and 200 drachmas to send us the photo we will never receive. We give him the money, just to get rid of him, then send him on his way. Sabrina is pissed off at me, but I'm already being drawn into the gates of the Acropolis, where she doesn't even exist.

I am nineteen years old and have been living in an apartment in a suburb of Athens for a year. From my kitchen window I can see the port of Piraeus while I wash my dishes. There is a marble balcony, the length of the entire apartment, where I can sit and watch the water and the blinking lights on the hills around me. It is my first apartment, and I love it thoroughly and unconditionally. It has only two rooms, but everything is new and compact, and the floors are made of pristine white marble. For the first time in my life, I become a neatnik, polishing my marble floor daily, sweeping away the marble dust so that my silhouette is mirrored in the shine day and night.

I live there for a year without a television or a phone, so entertainment is entirely up to me. Many strange and wonderful things are conjured up in the apartment. It is in the apartment that I fall madly, obsessively in love for the first time. Many horrible, traumatizing things happen in the apartment. It is there that I am first betrayed, drawn and quartered. I momentarily consider jumping off the marble balcony, but decorum saves me. I do not want to land in an embarrassing splayed position. If I can still imagine embarrassment after death, I assume this means that my will to live is still intact.

In my last weeks in the apartment, before moving to Holland with the man I will later marry then divorce, he and I go up to my roof to hang out laundry in the warm November sun. As I look out towards the sea, he calls me over and excitedly points at the Acropolis in the distance. I am thrilled, but do not admit that in all my time at the apartment, amidst poetry and heartbreak, music and heroin, I never noticed. I am happy that the Acropolis has been watching over me, my personal myth, my Greek tragedy, all this time. I wish I had seen it earlier. It would have comforted me.

In years to come, when I describe my first apartment, I always describe it with a view of the Acropolis—and everyone is impressed. I never say that I only saw it once.

I have come to Greece to make amends with my father, who I haven't spoken to in eight years. I am as stubborn and reticent, as walled-in as he is. It's amazing, the traits you can pick up without even being around someone. He wants me to fly directly to Heraklion in Crete, but I want to stop in Athens and gather a bit of my past. Bring it home and put the fragments together so I can start to understand what I'm made of. I take a book and walk up the hill to the Acropolis. At the gate I declare to the gatekeeper that I am a Greek woman, and that he should let me in for free. The socialists are in power, and one of their gifts to the Greek people is their heritage. No Greek pays to get into the Acropolis anymore. What type of Greek are you, the gatekeeper asks in amusement. A Cretan, I declare with a smile, and he waves me in.

There is a large sign by the gate announcing that a fifteen-year renovation project is underway, which will reverse the wear and tear and the pollution damage on the Acropolis. There is scaffolding everywhere and it feels as if I'm walking through a construction site where the buildings are half-built, not half-ruined. I'm happy to be there anyway and walk around grinning, looking for a place to sit and contemplate—somewhere where I won't be bothered by tourists. I overhear two young American women talking. One says to the other: "Not that impressive, is it?" I want to punch her, to yell in her face and ask her what her fucking country has done that even comes close to the grandeur, the nobility, and the wonder of the Acropolis. I imagine picking her up above my head and throwing her off the look-out point where the Greek flag flaps in the wind. But I don't. With a flick of my wrist, I dismiss her as a peasant, a fool, and I find a place to sit where the wind is calm, where the view is good. I sit there thinking for a few hours—content.

I have a red leather jacket that is my symbol of individuality—the leather worked-in and soft, the jacket comfortable and safe. It is destroyed in Crete by my father's mother, my insane grandmother Aglaia, an evil combination of ignorance and malice. She doesn't like the jacket and decides to do something about it, against everyone's warnings. She tosses it into her washing machine, turns on the hot water, and then says it was a mistake. When I call my mother in Montreal sobbing, she is as shocked and appalled at the violence of Aglaia's action as I am. She says that the jacket was to me as the Acropolis is to Greece. She is perfectly right. My father doesn't take my side.

In Toronto, where I now live, there is a cheese pie shop called the Acropolis Café. It is located on the Danforth—the long street that the Greek community has turned into a polis. The Danforth is dotted with restaurants, cafés, pastry shops, churches, and old Greek ladies in black complaining conversationally as they pick their vegetables from outdoor markets. I love cheese pies for breakfast and thrived on them when I lived in Greece. One of my Toronto lovers becomes a convert to all things Greek—he even tries to learn the language. There is an expression in Greek, meant to dissuade foreigners from picking up our tongue, that goes: "Greek is easy to learn—after the first ten years."

My lover drives me out to the Danforth for cheese pies on the odd Saturday. He says that I put on my Greek attitude the moment we set foot in the café—gruff, demanding, unsmiling. Demanding is the only defence against being taken for a fool when you deal with Greeks. They may not like you, but they won't fuck you over—won't give you stale cheese pies. They must know who they're dealing with. In my case they rarely do. Most Greek people don't recognize me as Greek and try to get away with things reserved for foreigners. I then have the pleasure of putting them in their place.

Two old Greek ladies are in the Acropolis Café eating cheese pies, drinking coffee, moaning about life. A group of young Greek men walk in, and there is a curt exchange between them and the old gals. After we leave, my lover comments upon how great it must be to be part of a community where people know each other and are bonded by their history, where old ladies and young men greet each other amicably.

"Are you kidding?" I reply. They weren't greeting each other. The old ladies were chastising the young men for leaving the café door open because, "Old people get cold." The men shot back that if they wanted the door closed, they could do it themselves. Then they made fun of my lover's earrings. Poor boy, WASP dreams dashed, becomes frightened of a culture where even old ladies don't take shit. He looks over at me, worried.

When I came back to Canada after my first trip to Greece, with my smuggled Acropolis stone, I visited my father's printing shop and proudly displayed my monumental souvenir. He frowned, as he often does when around me, and told me that if every visitor to the Acropolis took a stone, soon there would be no Acropolis left to visit. He recommended that I send it back. I didn't want to send it back, but I felt embarrassed and guilty, so I hid the stone somewhere, out of shame.

I'd like to report that I kept the stone until I grew up, and that I display it with pride next to my chunk of the Berlin wall, my piece of agate from the caves of West Virginia, and my grisgris bag from the Voodoo Museum in New Orleans—the things I have come to treasure as an adult. But the stone is lost. Mostly, you don't understand the value of things until they're gone, until you've grown enough to know what a monument to your existence the thing was, a marker on the path of your experience.

The last I remember seeing the stone was as a teenager. It was at the bottom of a make-up pouch, smudged with green eye pencil and red lipstick. For all I know, it was dropped in the toilet and flushed away with tissues and pencil shavings as I hurried out of the house for a date. Passed into the earth's bowels like a kidney stone.

TESS FRAGOULIS was born on the isle of Crete and emigrated to Canada with her parents in 1965. She was raised in Montreal as one of those increasingly rare birds—an Anglo-Greek- Montrealer. After several lost years spent in nightclubs in Montreal, Athens, and New York, she attended Concordia University, where she completed a B.A. in English before moving to Toronto in search of fame and fortune. Finding neither, she returned to Montreal, where she now lives. Her work has appeared in numerous magazines, journals, and anthologies, including *Canadian Fiction, Blood and Aphorisms, McGill Street, Quarry*, and *Venue*. She has also written for children's television. She is currently completing an M.A. in English and working on a novel.